Instructions to His Generals

The Military Philosophy of Frederick the Great

A Modern Translation

Adapted for the Contemporary Reader

Frederick the Great

Translated by Tim Zengerink

Table of Contents

Preface - Message to the Reader

Rebuilding the Greatest Library in Human History

Thousands of years ago, the Library of Alexandria was the heart of global knowledge — until it was lost.

Now, we're rebuilding it — and you're invited to join.

At the Modern Library of Alexandria, our mission is simple: make *every book* available to *every person*, in every language, format, and edition.

Here's how we do it:

- **Deluxe Print Editions at True Printing Cost** - Order paperbacks, hardcovers, or boxsets at the exact printing cost — no markup.

- **Unlimited Access to the Greatest Works** - Explore thousands of timeless classics in modern eBook and audiobook editions. Free for every reader, everywhere.

- **Modern Translations for Every Language & Dialect** -Clear, accessible versions of the world's greatest works, translated into every language and dialect.

When you visit **LibraryofAlexandria.com**, you're not just accessing books — you're joining a global movement to restore, preserve, and share the wisdom of civilization.

Join us today at LibraryofAlexandria.com

Together, we'll ensure the light of human wisdom never fades again.

With gratitude,

The Modern Library of Alexandria Team

Visit:

www.libraryofalexandria.com

Or scan the code below:

Introduction

"An army, like a serpent, moves on its belly."

~ Frederick the Great

The enduring legacy of *Instructions to His Generals* lies in its synthesis of precise military guidance and timeless strategic wisdom. Frederick the Great's insights emerged from a lifetime of experience as both a statesman and a military commander. His *Instructions to His Generals* reflect the mindset of a leader who understood the delicate balance between theory and practice, preparation and action. While grounded in the context of 18th- century warfare, Frederick II's principles remain deeply relevant to leaders, tacticians, and decision-makers today. His work also reflects the deeper philosophy of a ruler shaped by the Enlightenment—one who valued rationality, intellectual curiosity, and a deep understanding of human nature. Frederick II provides a versatile guide to strategy that transcends its original military purpose. Leaders in business, politics, and personal pursuits can all learn from his approach to preparation, adaptability, and decision-making. Frederick II's work speaks to the strategist in all of us: those who seek not only to overcome immediate obstacles but to outthink, outmaneuver, and inspire.

I. Frederick the Great: The King and Commander

A Life of Strategy and Leadership

Frederick II of Prussia, also known as Frederick the Great, was born in 1712 into a world that was both rigid and turbulent. His early life was defined by the strict upbringing imposed by his father, Frederick William I, a king notorious for his militaristic values and severe discipline. Young Frederick grew up under immense pressure, his days filled with rigorous military drills, harsh punishments, and constant surveillance. Frederick William I demanded obedience and despised intellectual pursuits, dismissing anything he considered unmanly or frivolous. Yet even in this stifling environment, Frederick displayed a keen intellect and a rebellious spirit. Frederick II's relationship with his father was marked by profound tension, leading him to flee Prussia as a young man. The escape failed, and Frederick was imprisoned, witnessing the execution of his closest friend as punishment for their plan. This traumatic episode became a turning point in Frederick II's life, forcing him to reconcile his intellectual passions with the harsh realities of power and leadership. Over time, he transformed from a reluctant heir into one of history's most formidable commanders—a leader who embodied both the ruthless pragmatism of his father and the enlightened ideals of his own generation.

When Frederick II ascended to the throne in 1740, Prussia was a relatively small kingdom surrounded by larger, more powerful empires. Within months of his reign, he launched an audacious military campaign to seize Silesia, a rich Austrian province. The decision shocked Europe, as it displayed not only Frederick's ambition but also his willingness to take calculated risks. Through a combination of bold tactics, strategic planning, and unrelenting determination, Frederick II secured Prussia's foothold in the region, marking the beginning of his transformation into a warrior-king.

The Historical Context of 18th-Century Europe

The Enlightenment was reshaping intellectual and cultural life, challenging traditional authority and emphasizing reason, progress, and individual liberty. At the same time, the political landscape was defined by fierce competition among powerful states: Austria, France, Britain, and Russia vied for dominance, while smaller nations like Prussia sought to carve out a place for themselves.

Prussia, under Frederick II's rule, emerged as a rising power in this volatile environment. The kingdom faced existential threats on all sides, from Austria's determination to reclaim Silesia to Russia's growing influence in Eastern Europe. Frederick II understood that Prussia's survival depended on its ability to punch above its weight—to outthink, outmaneuver, and outperform larger adversaries. This understanding shaped his approach to war and governance: he valued preparation, efficiency, and adaptability, recognizing that every resource and opportunity must be maximized to secure victory.

Frederick II's reign was defined by two major conflicts: the Silesian Wars (1740-1748) and the Seven Years' War (1756- 1763). These wars tested his leadership, strategy, and resilience, forcing him to confront overwhelming odds and find innovative ways to triumph. Frederick's ability to navigate these challenges solidified his reputation as one of history's greatest military minds.

Frederick's success on the battlefield stemmed from his ability to combine meticulous planning with tactical ingenuity. He understood that victory was not merely a matter of brute force but of strategic positioning, resource management, and psychological advantage. His leadership during the Silesian Wars showcased his boldness and creativity, as he employed rapid movements, surprise attacks, and unconventional tactics to defeat numerically superior forces.

The Seven Years' War presented an even greater challenge. Prussia faced a coalition of powerful enemies, including Austria, France, and Russia, who sought to crush Frederick II's ambitions and dismantle his kingdom. Outnumbered and surrounded, Frederick II relied on his ability to adapt to changing circumstances, exploit his opponents' weaknesses, and inspire his troops to persevere. Key victories, such as the Battle of Rossbach and the Battle of Leuthen, demonstrated Frederick II's mastery of maneuver warfare—the art of using speed, flexibility, and terrain to achieve decisive results.

Frederick II believed that discipline and preparation were the foundations of success, famously stating, "Soldiers must fear their officers more than the enemy." Yet Frederick II also understood the importance of trust and loyalty.

II How to read Instructions to His Generals

Written with the precision of a field marshal and the insight of a philosopher-king, its purpose is twofold: to ensure his generals were prepared for the responsibilities of command and to pass down hard-earned wisdom that could turn the tide of battle. Frederick II's experiences—gained through campaigns that tested his leadership, judgment, and endurance—are condensed into actionable advice. While the immediate audience for these instructions was his trusted officers, their relevance extends far beyond 18th-century battlefields. Modern readers can extract invaluable lessons on leadership, preparation, adaptability, and decision-making under pressure.

Frederick II's *Instructions to His Generals* capture this philosophy, addressing everything from the meticulous logistics that precede a campaign to the split-second decisions made amidst combat. The result is a work that reads as both a guide for military success and a broader reflection on the nature of leadership in high-stakes environments. He writes with clarity and directness, ensuring that his generals can grasp complex ideas quickly and apply them effectively. From organizing supply lines and maintaining troop morale to adapting tactics based on terrain and enemy movements, Frederick II covers every element that a commander must consider.

Flexibility, quick thinking, and the ability to seize fleeting opportunities are equally critical. In other sections, he issues cautionary warnings—urging commanders to avoid overconfidence, recklessness, and complacency. These reflections elevate the instructions from a technical manual to a timeless guide for navigating uncertainty and adversity.

The concise nature of Frederick II's writing is another of its strengths. For example, his emphasis on preparation and logistics is captured in what might be considered a precursor to the modern military adage: "Amateurs talk strategy; professionals talk logistics." Such statements are more than observations; they are directives that command attention and resonate far beyond their immediate context. The *Instructions to His Generals* offer a framework for thinking strategically, acting decisively, and leading effectively in any environment.

III Themes of Instructions to His Generals

The Importance of Preparation and Logistics

Frederick II warns his generals that neglecting these foundational elements invites disaster. Troops cannot fight without food, supplies, and well-maintained equipment. An army that runs out of provisions is already defeated. Frederick II's emphasis on preparation reflects his pragmatic understanding of warfare. He saw logistics as a decisive factor in any campaign. By ensuring that his forces were well-equipped and provisioned, he created the conditions for success while limiting the risk of failure.

While Frederick II valued preparation, he also recognized that war is inherently unpredictable. Circumstances change, plans unravel, and unexpected challenges arise. For this reason, he emphasized the importance of flexibility and adaptability. Commanders, he argued, must be ready to adjust their tactics to match the realities of the battlefield, exploiting enemy weaknesses and seizing opportunities as they appear.

Frederick II's approach to adaptability is best illustrated in his advocacy for maneuver warfare. By remaining agile and responsive, his forces could gain decisive advantages even against numerically superior enemies. This principle of adaptability extends beyond the battlefield. Leaders in any field must learn to think on their feet, adjust their plans, and capitalize on changing circumstances.

These core themes—preparation, adaptability, discipline, intelligence, resourcefulness, morale, and balance—form the foundation of Frederick the Great's philosophy of leadership and strategy. Together, they offer a timeless framework for navigating the challenges of warfare, leadership, and decision-making. While Frederick wrote for his generals, his insights resonate far beyond the battlefield, providing valuable lessons for anyone striving to lead effectively, think strategically, and achieve success in the face of uncertainty.

Learning to Think Like a General

To "think like a general" is to learn Frederick II's approach to leadership, strategy, and decision-making. He approached every challenge from multiple angles, analyzing the environment, anticipating opponents' moves, and positioning his forces to exploit opportunities. Frederick II was not reactive; he was proactive. He emphasized the importance of information and understanding the broader dynamics at play. Leaders who learn to think in this way can anticipate challenges, identify patterns, and craft winning strategies.

IV Translating Instructions to His Generals to Modern Readers

The voice of Frederick the Great—sharp, direct, and authoritative—is at the heart of these works. This translation preserves that voice with great care, balancing faithfulness to the original text with accessibility for contemporary readers. His words are purposeful, and this translation maintains that intent, ensuring that the reader can experience his clarity and command as it was meant to be. His tone remains firm and unyielding, his insights as piercing and relevant as ever. By carefully adapting his words for a contemporary audience, this version allows Frederick II's brilliance to shine through without unnecessary barriers. Whether you are leading a team, managing a business, or striving for personal growth, these works offer tools to navigate complex situations with confidence and clarity.

THE KING OF PRUSSIA'S MILITARY

Instructions to His Generals

ARTICLE I

REGARDING PRUSSIANTROOPS: THEIR STRENGTHS AND WEAKNESSES

To shape and maintain my troops, commanding officers must exercise the highest degree of diligence and care. Absolute discipline is essential, and attention to their well-being must be a priority. Prussian soldiers deserve a standard of nourishment superior to that of almost any other European army.

Our regiments are half-composed of native soldiers and half of foreign enlistees who join for financial gain. The latter often seek any opportunity to leave a service to which they hold no personal allegiance, making the prevention of desertion a vital concern.

Some of our generals mistakenly assume that one soldier can replace another without consequence, as long as the ranks are filled. But this view fails to recognize the unique conditions of our own army compared to others. If a deserter is replaced by a soldier equally trained and disciplined, the impact may be minimal. However, if a soldier who has two years of training deserts and is replaced by a poorly trained recruit— or left unreplaced—the effect on the regiment can be significant.

Such lapses in officer vigilance have, at times, led to regiments not only losing personnel but also diminishing in reputation. When regiments lose disciplined soldiers, the army itself weakens precisely when full strength is most needed. Without dedicated effort, you risk losing the best of your forces and may find it challenging to restore your ranks.

While Prussia has a healthy population, finding men of the necessary height for service is no simple task. Even if they are available, they cannot be trained immediately. For this reason, preventing desertion becomes one of the essential responsibilities of generals commanding armies or detachments. To achieve this:

1. Avoid encamping too close to forests unless absolutely necessary.

2. Conduct roll calls several times each day.

3. Send hussar patrols frequently to scout the area surrounding the camp.

4. Station chasseurs in crop fields at night and double cavalry posts at dusk to secure the perimeter.

5. Do not allow soldiers to stray and ensure that each unit is led to water and forage by an officer.

6. Enforce strict punishment for marauding, as it breeds disorder.

7. Keep guards stationed in villages until the troops are assembled on marching days.

8. Enforce strict orders prohibiting any soldier from leaving his rank or division while on the march.

9. Avoid night marches unless absolutely necessary.

10. Deploy hussar patrols on both flanks while infantry move through wooded areas.

11. Position officers at both ends of a defile to maintain order in ranks.

12. If a backward march becomes necessary, keep the reason concealed from the troops, or offer a motivating explanation to maintain morale.

13. **Ensure regular provision of essential supplies** such as bread, meat, beer, brandy, and other necessities for the troops. Maintaining a steady and dependable issue of these is crucial for morale and health.

14. **Identify the root causes of desertion** if it begins to affect a regiment or company. Investigate whether the soldiers have received their enlistment bonuses and customary benefits, and determine if any misconduct by captains or officers might be a contributing factor. However, under

no circumstances should discipline be relaxed. Some may believe that this is the responsibility of the colonel alone, yet the efforts of one individual cannot suffice to achieve excellence across the entire force. An army must strive collectively for cohesion and unity, giving the impression of being directed by a single, resolute mind.

An army is largely composed of individuals who, if not under consistent direction, may tend toward idleness. Without vigilant oversight from the general, who enforces a strong sense of duty, this carefully assembled force will begin to deteriorate, losing its effectiveness and ultimately becoming little more than the semblance of a disciplined army. For this reason, **constant, purposeful activity for the troops** is essential. Commanders who maintain such discipline will see the clear benefits, and they will also notice that numerous minor infractions often go unaddressed by those who lack the vigilance to uncover and address them.

Although this level of continuous attention may initially seem burdensome for a general, the substantial rewards make it well worthwhile. With troops of such exceptional bravery, skill, and discipline, the achievements possible are boundless. A general who may appear reckless or overly bold in other nations would, with our troops, be considered merely diligent in adhering to established standards. With a force of well-provisioned soldiers like ours, any undertaking within human capability can be approached with confidence. Furthermore, the soldiers uphold such a high standard that anyone showing signs of cowardice or hesitation would not be tolerated among them, a stance rarely seen in other armies.

I have personally observed officers and soldiers alike who, even when severely wounded, would not abandon their post or retreat to seek medical attention. With troops of this quality, almost any objective becomes attainable. Supplied adequately, they are capable of incredible feats. Whether marching at a rapid pace to gain an advantage over the enemy, storming a forest position, scaling a mountain, or engaging in cavalry charges, they exhibit unshakable courage and resilience. In close combat, they will press on relentlessly, turning resistance into rout and transforming a mere encounter into a decisive victory.

However, the excellence of the troops alone is not enough. The general's expertise is equally vital, as the incompetence or poor judgment of leadership can squander all advantages. Therefore, I will now discuss the essential qualities that a general must possess. I will also outline specific principles and guidelines, whether derived from the wisdom of experienced generals or from hard-won lessons learned through my own experience.

ARTICLE II

ON TROOP SUBSISTENCE AND PROVISIONING

A notable general once remarked that feeding an army should be its foundational priority, as it sustains all operations. This crucial aspect can be divided into two sections: the first addresses where and how to establish supply depots, while the second covers the effective use and transport of these supplies.

The foremost rule is to establish large supply depots securely in the rear of the army whenever possible. During the wars in Silesia and Bohemia, our main depot was located in Breslau, strategically chosen for its access to replenishment via the Oder River. Establishing depots directly at the front lines may seem efficient, but a single setback could force their abandonment, leaving the army without resources. When depots are organized sequentially in the rear, any operational setback will only be a temporary obstacle rather than a full-scale crisis.

On the Electorate's frontiers, the most strategic locations for depots would be Spandau and Magdeburg, with the latter's position on the Elbe particularly suited for offensive campaigns into Saxony. For operations toward Bohemia, Schweidnitz would be an ideal location.

The integrity of commissaries and their deputies is crucial in this regard, as dishonest conduct directly compromises the state. Therefore, officials of reputable character should be appointed to these positions, and they should regularly conduct personal and meticulous inspections to verify accuracy in all records.

There are two primary methods of stocking depots: one is to procure grain by purchasing it from local nobility and peasants at established finance chamber rates; the other method is through requisitioning specified quantities. Commissaries are responsible for coordinating and authorizing these transactions.

Specially constructed vessels should be used to transport grain and forage along rivers and canals. However, purveyors should only be hired under the most pressing circumstances since even Jewish merchants, known for demanding high prices, are typically more reasonable. Purveyors' inflated rates drive up the costs of supplies, which they then resell at extravagant profits.

Supply depots must be prepared well in advance so that the army has everything it needs when setting out on campaign. Delaying their establishment until winter could mean that freezing conditions halt river transport, or that roads become so bogged down that transporting supplies becomes exceedingly difficult.

In addition to the covered wagons assigned to regiments, which carry an eight-day bread supply, the commissary has provisions for transporting a month's worth of supplies. The use of navigable waterways should never be overlooked; without this transport option, no army can be reliably or abundantly supplied.

Wagons used for transporting supplies should be drawn exclusively by horses. Attempts have been made to use oxen, but they proved inadequate. Wagon masters must pay careful attention to the well-being of their animals, as the loss of horses directly reduces the number of wagons, thereby diminishing the army's provisions. The general must also oversee this matter since neglected horses mean fewer wagons and potentially lost supplies on the march. Inadequately fed or exhausted horses will inevitably falter, leading to a breakdown in logistics and possibly derailing well-planned operations. Thus, the general must diligently monitor these essential factors, which are critical to the success of all military maneuvers.

When conducting a campaign against Saxony, using the Elbe River to transport provisions is highly advantageous. In Silesia, the Oder serves this purpose, while in Prussia, access to the sea is invaluable. However, in Bohemia and Moravia, land transport is the sole means of conveyance. Often, a line of depots is created, as in Bohemia in 1742, when magazines were established at Pardubitz, Nienbourg, Podjebrod, and Brandies. This chain enabled us to keep pace with the enemy and pursue him toward Prague if necessary. Similarly, in the recent Bohemian campaign, Breslau supplied Schweidnitz, which in turn supplied Jaromirez, and from there provisions were carried directly to the army.

In addition to the covered wagons carrying provisions, the army transports portable iron ovens, which have recently been increased in number. These ovens are set up during rest days to bake fresh bread. On any expedition, it's essential to carry a ten-day supply of bread or biscuits. While biscuits are an excellent ration, our soldiers are not accustomed to utilizing them efficiently and typically only enjoy them in soup form.

When marching through hostile territory, the meal depot should be kept in a secure, garrisoned town near the army. For instance, in the 1745 campaign, our depots progressed from Neustadt to Jaromirez and eventually to Trautenau. If our advance had extended further, our nearest secure depot would have been at Pardubitz. Each company has been provided with hand mills, which have proven invaluable. These mills are operated by soldiers who grind the meal, exchange it at the depot, and receive bread in return. This setup allows us to conserve larger stores and remain in camp longer than would otherwise be possible, reducing the need for large escorts and frequent convoys.

Regarding convoy security, I must elaborate. The strength of the escort should match the anticipated threat level from the enemy. Infantry detachments are stationed in towns along the convoy route, providing support points. Sometimes, large covering detachments are deployed, as was done in Bohemia. In terrain with significant cover, infantry should primarily compose convoy escorts, supplemented with hussars to scout for hidden enemy positions and survey the route.

Even in open terrain, I favor infantry over cavalry for convoy escorts, as I find them more effective in this role. For details on convoy escort procedures, I direct you to my military regulations. Securing convoys should be a high priority for the general. One reliable strategy is to deploy troops to occupy key defiles before the convoy reaches them and position the escort a league ahead of the convoy toward the enemy's position. This maneuver effectively masks the convoy, allowing it to pass securely through challenging areas.

ARTICLE III

OF SUTLERS, BEER, AND BRANDY.

When planning any operation against the enemy, it is essential to direct the commissary to gather all available beer and brandy to ensure the army has these supplies, at least for the initial days. As soon as the army crosses into enemy territory, all nearby brewers and distillers must be requisitioned at once. Distillers, in particular, should be set to work immediately so that soldiers won't miss out on their rations, which they rely on greatly for morale.

Sutlers must be protected, especially in areas where local inhabitants have fled and where regular provisions cannot be obtained with money. In such instances, we have some leeway to avoid strict adherence to local regulations concerning the peasantry. The sutlers and accompanying women should be sent to search for vegetables and livestock to supplement rations. Attention must be paid to the prices of provisions, ensuring that soldiers can buy supplies at fair prices while allowing sutlers to earn a reasonable profit.

It's worth noting that during a campaign, soldiers receive two pounds of bread daily and two pounds of meat weekly at no charge—a privilege they greatly deserve, particularly in regions like Bohemia, where the terrain is harsh and resources are limited.

Convoys transporting supplies for the army should also include herds of cattle to guarantee soldiers' nourishment and sustain their strength throughout the campaign.

ARTICLE IV

OF DRY AND GREEN FORAGE.

Dry forage includes items like oats, barley, hay, and chopped straw, which are stored in the magazine. If the oats are spoiled or musty, the horses are likely to develop mange or farcy, rendering them weak and ineffective even at the beginning of a campaign. Although chopped straw is traditionally given, it merely serves to fill the belly without providing substantial nourishment.

The initial aim of gathering and storing forage is to ensure a strategic advantage, either by preparing ahead of the enemy or by stocking up for a distant campaign. However, when horses are limited to dry forage, the army often cannot afford to stray too far from its supply magazines due to the sheer challenge of transporting enough feed; entire regions sometimes lack sufficient carriages to meet the army's needs. Consequently, this approach is usually reserved for situations lacking rivers to facilitate the transportation of forage.

During the Silesian campaign, my cavalry was entirely reliant on dry forage, but we limited our movement from Strehla to Schwiednitz (where there was a magazine) and onward to Cracau, where we were near the Brieg and Oder Rivers. For winter campaigns, cavalry should carry forage sufficient for five days, firmly bound on their mounts—particularly if action is anticipated in regions like Bohemia or Moravia, where inadequate forage would rapidly weaken the horses.

In regions with standing crops or unharvested fields, forage is gathered there first, moving to village stores only when the fields are exhausted. When the army plans to remain in one location, an inventory of available forage should be taken to ensure that rations are distributed evenly according to the intended duration of stay.

For large foraging operations, the escort typically consists of a body of cavalry sized according to proximity to the enemy and the perceived threat level. In some instances, entire wings or even the entire army may engage in foraging activities.

Foragers assemble on their designated routes, positioned on the army's wings, front, or rear as necessary. Hussars lead the advance, followed by cavalry in open terrain; in rougher areas, infantry precedes the cavalry. This advanced guard moves ahead of the main foraging column, which is divided into sections. Each section of foragers is followed by an escort composed of both horse and foot soldiers. This staggered arrangement continues, with successive detachments of foragers and escort troops. The rear guard comprises a final troop of hussars, completing the orderly formation and protecting the column's tail.

It is important to remember that all escorts should have infantry carrying their cannons and foragers equipped with swords and carbines. Upon reaching the designated foraging area, a protective chain must be set up, positioning infantry near villages, behind hedges, or in sunken paths. A reserve unit combining cavalry and infantry should be centrally located, ready to provide support at any vulnerable points where the enemy might attempt to break through. The hussars are to engage in skirmishes with the enemy to create distractions and draw them away from the foragers. Once the area is secured, the foraging ground is divided among regiments, and officers must ensure that foraged bundles are tightly bound and large enough to maximize the load.

When the horses are loaded, the foragers should return to camp in small groups, each protected by an escort. Once the foragers have vacated the area, the chain troops should gather to form the rear guard, with the hussars following behind to provide additional cover.

Foraging in villages follows a similar procedure, with the key difference being that infantry form a defensive perimeter around the village while the cavalry holds a position slightly behind, ready to act if necessary. Each village should be foraged individually to avoid overly dispersing the chain troops.

In mountainous regions, foraging becomes a challenging operation, requiring escorts primarily composed of infantry and hussars due to the rugged terrain. When camped close to the enemy for an extended period, it's essential to secure the forage located between both camps first. Foraging should then extend outward up to two leagues, beginning with the more distant fields and reserving those nearest to camp for later use. If the army doesn't plan to stay long, foraging can focus on the immediate camp area and surroundings.

When gathering a substantial amount of green forage, it's preferable to send out smaller foraging parties twice rather than spread across too wide an area all at once. This strategy keeps the protective chain more compact and the foragers safer, as stretching the chain too thinly weakens it, making it vulnerable to being breached by the enemy.

ARTICLE V

OF THE KNOWLEDGE OF A COUNTRY.

Understanding the geography of a country is essential and can be acquired through two primary methods. The first step is to thoroughly study a map of the anticipated war zone, clearly noting the names of significant rivers, towns, and mountains. This preliminary step helps create a general framework of the area. With this groundwork established, the next phase involves a more detailed examination to understand the layout of major roads, the locations of towns, and whether these towns can be fortified for defense or how best to attack them if the enemy occupies them. The defense requirements for these towns should also be assessed.

It's crucial to have accurate plans of fortified towns to understand their defenses and identify the most vulnerable points. Equally important is the knowledge of rivers, including their depth, navigability, and any potential crossing points, along with seasonal changes—whether rivers are impassable in spring or dry up in summer. Marshes, which could hinder movement, should also be identified.

In a flat, open landscape, fertile areas should be

distinguished from barren ones, and it's important to know the possible routes connecting major cities and rivers, including how to secure camps along these routes. Flat areas are easily surveyed; however, in mountainous or forested regions, where visibility is limited, reconnaissance is more challenging. To gather essential information in such terrains, it's helpful to climb high points with a map in hand and bring along local villagers, such as hunters or shepherds, who know the area. If a single mountain stands taller than others, it should be ascended to gain a comprehensive view of the area of interest.

Familiarity with roads is critical—not only to plan marching formations but also to strategize alternative routes for reaching or flanking the enemy's camp should they establish nearby positions. Identifying defensive camps, potential battlefields, and enemy- held posts are among the most important reconnaissance goals.

Each reconnaissance should yield a complete understanding of key locations, valleys, defiles, and all advantageous sites. Every possible action should be carefully considered to create well- prepared arrangements, eliminating confusion when action is required. These preparations should be meticulous, revisited and revised as needed, until they are entirely satisfactory.

When choosing camps for either offense or defense, it is generally essential to ensure proximity to wood and water, a well-shielded front, and an open rear. If a thorough personal inspection of the area is not possible, intelligent, resourceful officers should be dispatched, under plausible pretexts or even in disguise if necessary, to gather the necessary intelligence. They must know precisely what to observe, and upon their return, their findings on potential camps and other locations should be added to the map. However, where possible, personal reconnaissance is always preferable over secondhand accounts.

ARTICLE VI

OF THE COUP D'OEIL.

Understanding the coup d'oeil in military strategy can be broken down into two primary skills. The first is the ability to accurately assess how many troops a specific area can hold. This skill only develops through practice; after overseeing the layout of several camps, the eye becomes attuned to space, so estimation errors become minimal.

The second, and more critical skill, is the ability to identify immediately all possible advantages of any piece of ground. While some may seem naturally adept at this, it is a skill that can be learned and perfected. Fortification principles are the foundation of this skill, providing a universal framework adaptable to any army's position. With this knowledge, an experienced general can utilize every defile, marsh, hollow path, or slight rise in terrain to their advantage.

In a space of two square leagues, there might be two hundred potential positions to consider, yet an insightful general will quickly identify the most advantageous one. This begins with examining even small elevations to get a comprehensive view of the surroundings. Using the same fortification principles, the general can pinpoint the weaknesses in the enemy's formation. Ideally, if time allows, the general should walk over the ground to become even more familiar with the terrain.

Fortification principles also guide how to occupy heights effectively, ensuring positions are not easily dominated by higher ground nearby. These principles provide insight on how to secure the wings so the flanks are well-covered, and they also aid in distinguishing strong, defensible positions from those that would be difficult and risky to hold, even for a seasoned leader. Through this approach, a general can also recognize weaknesses in the enemy's setup, whether due to a poorly chosen position, an ill- judged distribution of forces, or limited natural defenses.

These considerations naturally lead into how troops should be arranged to maximize the benefits of their environment, which I will outline next.

ARTICLE VII

OF THE DISTRIBUTION OF TROOPS

While understanding and selecting suitable terrain is crucial, it's equally important to make full use of these advantages so that each unit is positioned where it can be most effective. Cavalry, known for its speed, should be deployed on open ground to maximize maneuverability, while infantry can handle a wider range of terrain, using their firepower for defense and bayonets for offense. Defensive measures are typically established first to ensure a camp's security, particularly in areas where an enemy engagement is possible at any moment.

Current battle formations are often inherited from earlier strategies and don't always consider the unique features of the terrain. This can lead to a misapplication of tactics. The entire army should be arranged according to what each segment of terrain demands. For example, while plains may suit cavalry, if a plain is small or bordered by woods with enemy infantry positioned there, then cavalry may need to be placed at the edges of the infantry wings to benefit from their support.

There are cases where all cavalry might be positioned on one wing or held in reserve. At other times, infantry brigades may close off their wings. Ideal locations for troops include elevated areas, churchyards, sunken roads, or broad ditches. When used wisely, such terrain features can effectively shield against attacks.

However, placing cavalry behind a swamp or marsh limits their usefulness, as they would be unable to charge effectively. Similarly, positioning cavalry too close to wooded areas could allow enemy forces to cause disarray from cover. Infantry faces similar risks when placed on open ground without protected flanks, as the enemy will likely exploit such vulnerabilities by attacking the exposed side.

In mountainous terrain, I would position the cavalry in the second line, deploying only a few squadrons in the first line for support or for flanking any enemy infantry attempting to advance. Generally, well-organized armies form a cavalry reserve on open plains, while in broken or uneven landscapes, this reserve typically consists of infantry with some light cavalry, such as hussars and dragoons.

The art of troop deployment lies in positioning each unit so it can perform optimally and contribute uniformly to the operation. Villeroi's error at the Battle of Ramillies illustrates this: by stationing his left wing behind an impassable swamp, he prevented it from supporting his right wing, thereby losing the utility of a significant portion of his force. This oversight demonstrates how critical it is to ensure that each unit's placement allows for effective maneuvering and support.

ARTICLE VIII

OF CAMPS

To ensure your camp is well-chosen, assess whether a minor movement on your part forces the enemy into a more substantial shift, or if, after one of your marches, they are compelled to make additional ones. The side with the fewest necessary maneuvers is generally in the better position.

The responsibility for selecting the camp's location should rest solely with the general, as the chosen spot often becomes the battlefield, and the success of his operations hinges on this decision. Given the importance of this matter, I'll delve into it in detail, focusing solely on factors that directly impact the general and leaving the specific placement of troops within the camp to my military regulation.

Camps serve two primary functions: defense and preparation for attack. The first type includes camps where troops are gathered primarily for rest and convenience, ideally near the magazine but organized so they can quickly form a battle line. These camps should generally be positioned at a distance from the enemy to avoid disturbances. Ignoring this caution, as the King of England did by encamping along the bank of the Main opposite the French army, led to a significant risk of defeat at Dettingen.

The first essential rule when selecting a camp location is proximity to both wood and water. In our custom, camps are fortified, following the Roman example, to guard against possible surprise attacks by enemy light troops and to discourage desertion. I've noticed consistently fewer instances of desertion when the camp's defenses were solid, such as when redans were interconnected by two lines extending around the perimeter, as opposed to camps without this added security. This may seem trivial but has proven to be a substantial factor in maintaining troop integrity.

Camps of rest, intended for provisioning and observation, are another type. These camps are positioned to monitor enemy movements without being actively engaged, allowing us to respond to their maneuvers. Since relaxation is key in such camps, they are often located behind large rivers, marshes, or other natural barriers that make their front impassable. Our camp at Strehla, for instance, was of this type. When streams or rivers at the camp's front are too shallow, they should be dammed to increase their depth.

Even in camps of this nature, where the enemy threat is minimal, the general must remain vigilant. The time granted here should be used to oversee the troops closely and restore discipline. The general should verify that operations proceed according to protocol, ensuring officers on guard understand and fulfill their responsibilities, and confirm that the standards I've established for positioning cavalry and infantry guards are meticulously observed.

The infantry should undergo their drills three times each week, with new recruits practicing daily; at times, whole corps may execute their maneuvers together. The cavalry should also perform their exercises unless they're engaged in foraging, and the general, who is well-aware of each corps' exact numbers, must ensure that both the young soldiers and inexperienced horses are trained thoroughly. Regular visits to the lines are essential, where the general commends officers diligent with their troops and firmly reprimands those who show signs of neglect, as no large army can sustain itself without active supervision. Armies will inevitably be populated with idle or malingering soldiers who require the general's vigilance to stay engaged in their duties.

Camps like these yield great benefit if used as recommended, as the discipline and structure instilled in them lay a solid foundation for the upcoming campaign's success.

When we establish camp for foraging or other purposes, whether near the enemy or farther off, I will focus on the scenarios when we camp close to enemy lines. Here, choosing fertile grounds and strategically advantageous spots, either by natural terrain or fortified by human efforts, is essential.

Foraging camps positioned near the enemy should be difficult to reach, as foraging missions function like combat detachments sent against the opposition. These teams might encompass as much as one-sixth or even half the army, making it imperative that our location protects against any advantage the enemy might seize during these expeditions. A well-chosen camp can prevent these vulnerabilities.

However, even when our camp is well-positioned and appears secure, we cannot overlook further precautions. We must uphold strict secrecy about the timing and location of foraging missions, and not even the general assigned to lead these efforts should know the details until late the night before.

Sending out multiple scout parties is advisable to monitor any movements from the enemy; unless there are significant reasons against it, we might choose to forage on the same day as they do, though we must remain cautious. The enemy, learning of our intentions, might halt their own foraging and redirect their forces to attack our main group.

An example is Prince Charles of Lorraine's camp near Königgrätz, which was naturally fortified and ideal for foraging purposes. Similarly, our camp at Cholm became robust through human intervention, with abatis placed along the right wing and redoubts erected in front of the infantry camp to reinforce our defenses.

We entrench camps when preparing for a siege, defending a challenging passage, or compensating for terrain disadvantages by constructing defensive works to guard against potential enemy aggression.

When establishing entrenchments, a general should use every marsh, river, inundation, and natural or artificial obstruction to limit the width of defensive lines. It's better to construct smaller, manageable entrenchments rather than excessively large ones, as these barriers alone do not stop the enemy; it is the troops stationed behind them that prevent their advancement.

I would avoid constructing entrenchments unless I had sufficient battalions to line them continuously and a reserve of infantry that could be readily moved to any threatened point. Abbatis and other such barriers are useful only when actively defended by infantry.

The main focus should be on properly reinforcing the lines of countervallation, which typically end at a river. In such cases, the trench should extend into the river itself and be deepened enough to prevent fording; neglecting this precaution risks having your flank turned. Additionally, it's crucial to secure ample provisions before settling behind defensive lines to lay siege.

Entrenchments' flanks demand particular attention, as no segment should allow the enemy to approach without being subjected to crossfire from multiple directions. When defending mountain passes or defiles, entrenchments must be reinforced with extra caution, as support for the flanks is vital. Redoubts are often constructed on both wings, and sometimes the entire entrenchment comprises redoubts, ensuring that the defending troops are shielded from being outflanked.

Experienced generals skillfully direct the enemy to attack the most fortified points, where trenches are widened and deepened, lined with palisades, with chevaux de frise at entry points, and parapets made cannon-resistant. Additionally, pits are dug in vulnerable areas to further complicate enemy advances.

However, when it comes to covering a siege, I would always prefer deploying an army of observation over relying solely on an entrenched camp. This is simply because experience has shown that the old approach cannot be fully trusted. Prince de Condé saw his entrenchments before Arras overcome by Turenne, and if I recall correctly, Condé in turn broke through the entrenchments that Turenne had set up before Valenciennes. Since then, neither of these seasoned commanders relied on entrenched camps to cover sieges but opted instead for armies of observation.

I will now discuss defensive camps, which are naturally strong due to their position and meant solely to withstand enemy attacks. To make these positions serve their purpose effectively, the front and both flanks must be equally fortified, while the rear remains open and accessible. Ideal examples include elevated areas with extensive fronts and flanks protected by marshes, like Prince Charles of Lorraine's camp at Marschwitz, which was shielded by a marshy river in the front and lakes on the flanks, or our encampment at Konopist in 1744.

An alternative defensive measure is positioning near a fortified town, as demonstrated by Marshal de Neipperg after his defeat at Mollwitz when he took a secure position under the walls of Neiss. As long as a general can hold such a position, he remains secure from direct attack. However, if the enemy begins maneuvers to outflank him, he can no longer safely remain there. His preparations should, therefore, include fallback plans so that, if outflanked, he can retreat to another strong defensive position further back.

The geography of Bohemia, filled with naturally fortified spots, often forces us to occupy these camps, sometimes against our preference, due to the varied landscape that makes strategic maneuvering challenging.

I must reiterate the utmost importance of a general maintaining vigilance to avoid being lured into errors due to poorly chosen positions. A misjudgment in selecting posts could lead to situations where retreat is only possible through narrow, vulnerable defiles. If faced with a skillful opponent, a general could find himself so tightly confined and restricted by the terrain that he may have no option but to accept the most humiliating fate for a soldier: laying down arms without a chance to fight back.

In camps meant to defend a region, the priority should not be on the strength of the camp itself but on safeguarding the key points vulnerable to attack through which the enemy could breach. Such points should be secured by the camp's positioning. This doesn't mean occupying every possible approach an enemy might take, but rather the one route that would most likely lead to their objective. Selecting a strategic post allows us to thwart their plans, forcing them into extended detours while enabling us to disrupt their advances with minimal repositioning.

For example, the camp at Neustadt is strategically

placed to protect the entirety of Lower Silesia from an army stationed in Moravia. The ideal positioning involves having Neustadt and the river in front. Should the enemy attempt to move between Ottmachau and Glatz, we only need to shift our position between Neiss and Ziegenhals, where we can secure a favorable post that blocks them from accessing Moravia. Similarly, the enemy would hesitate to move toward Cosel because positioning ourselves between Troppau and Jaegerndorff—areas with numerous excellent strongholds— would sever their connection to supply convoys.

Another essential camp lies between Liebau and Schaemberg, providing Lower Silesia with formidable defense against threats from Bohemia. In all these scenarios, adherence to the principles I've outlined is vital, though, of course, flexibility in applying them to specific circumstances remains necessary. Additionally, when there's a river before our position, it's crucial to ensure that tents remain no farther than half musket-shot from the front of the camp, keeping defensive readiness intact.

As for the Brandenburg frontier, no camp alone can cover this open terrain, which spans six leagues of uninterrupted plains. Protecting it from Saxony demands control over Wittenberg, either by setting up camp there or following the approach taken in the winter expedition of 1745. The camp at Werben, on the other hand, serves effectively to secure the flank facing Hanover.

In offensive camps, it is essential to have both the front and flanks well fortified. If the flanks, typically the weakest points of an army, are not secured, confidence in the troops will falter. Our camp at Czaslaw, before the 1742 battle, suffered due to this very oversight. Additionally, villages positioned on the wings or in the camp's front are generally garrisoned by our troops, except on combat days when these troops are withdrawn. This precaution prevents potential hazards if the enemy sets these nearby wooden buildings—typical of the region—ablaze, risking loss of men. However, an exception to this rule can be made for villages with solid stone buildings or churchyards detached from flammable structures, as these can provide a defensible position without excessive risk.

Our main principle is to always be on the offensive, not defensive. This kind of position should only be held at the front of the army or in front of its wings; in these places, it will provide a lot of cover for our troops during an attack and will also be very troubling for the enemy throughout the fight.

It's also extremely important to check the depth of the small rivers or marshes that are in front of or on the flanks of our camp. Otherwise, if the rivers can be crossed or the marshes can be passed through, you might realize too late that you've trusted a weak point for defense. Villars was defeated at Malplaquet because he thought the marsh on his right couldn't be crossed, only to find it was just a dry meadow that our troops crossed easily to attack him from the side. Every detail should be inspected with our own eyes, and no matter of this kind should ever be ignored or treated as unimportant.

The front of the first line should be protected by infantry regiments, and if there is a river nearby, guards should be stationed on its banks. The back of the camp should be guarded by guards from the second line. These guards should be protected by simple redoubts joined by light earthworks, so the camp will be defended in the Roman style. We should occupy any villages located on the wings or even half a league away if they can help secure other access points.

The cavalry guards should be set up according to the rules I've outlined in my military instructions. We rarely had more than 300 maîtres de garde among 80 squadrons, unless we were very close to the enemy, as when we marched to Schweidnitz after the Battle of Hohenfriedberg, or when we entered Lusatia on our way to Naumbourg. These advance guards should include all types of troops, such as 2,000 hussars, 1,500 dragoons, and 2,000 grenadiers. The general commanding the forward troops should be a person with good judgment, and since his goal is to gather intelligence and not to engage in combat, his camps should be chosen with care, with woods or narrow passes he is familiar with positioned at the front. He should also send out regular patrols to gather information so that he knows at all times what is happening in the enemy's camp.

Meanwhile, if you use the hussars remaining with you to patrol the rear and the sides of the camp, you've taken every possible measure to protect against any hostile actions. If a large enemy force tries to slip between you and your rear guard, you can be sure they intend to attack it, and you should rush to provide support.

To sum up all I have to say on this topic, it's essential to add that if generals who set up their troops in villages want to be safe from danger and disturbance, they should only occupy villages located between the two main lines.

ARTICLE IX

IN WHAT MANNER AND FOR WHAT REASON WE ARE TO SEND OUT DETACHMENTS.

In war, there's an old saying: "He who divides his force will be beaten in detail." This advice has stood the test of time for a reason. If you're about to engage in battle, it's essential to bring together as many troops as you can, using every effort to gather as large a force as possible. When united, these troops can serve the best purpose in the upcoming fight. History has shown repeatedly that generals who overlook this rule usually find themselves with plenty of regret.

For instance, Albemarle's detachment at Oudenarde was defeated, which cost the great Eugene the entire campaign. Similarly, General Stahrenberg was defeated in the Battle of Villa Viciosa in Spain because he was separated from the English forces, unable to coordinate in time. These aren't isolated cases. Detached forces have repeatedly caused disastrous losses, as seen in the Austrian campaigns in Hungary. Prince Hildburghausen's army suffered defeat at Banja Luka, and General Wallis was dealt a setback on the Timok River's banks. The Saxons, too, were beaten at Kesselsdorf due to their failure to unite with Prince Charles, even though circumstances allowed for it. Personally, I nearly faced defeat at Sohr; it was only the quick thinking of my generals and the courageous action of my soldiers that saved me from such a fate. Had they faltered, I would have paid the price for having fragmented forces.

This leads to an important question: should detachments never be sent out under any circumstances? My response is that detaching forces is a sensitive decision and should only be made under the most urgent necessity and for reasons of the highest importance. When conducting an offensive, sending out detachments should generally be avoided. Even in open country where you may control a few locations, only the minimum number of troops should be spared to protect supply convoys, and no more. Keeping your force unified is paramount.

However, there are exceptions, particularly in specific regions such as Bohemia or Moravia. In these areas, the need for provisions can make it necessary to send out detachments to ensure the arrival of supplies. Encampments should be set up along the chain of mountains where supply convoys must pass. These encampments should remain in place until you've gathered enough supplies to sustain the army for several months. Additionally, securing a strong position within the enemy's territory as a supply depot becomes crucial. Once these detachments are deployed, the main army should move into advantageous camps and wait for their safe return.

An advanced guard, however, should not be considered a detachment. The purpose of an advanced guard is to stay in close proximity to the main army. Under no circumstances should it be stationed too close to the enemy, as its function is not to be exposed to undue risk.

In some cases, particularly when on the defensive, there may be no choice but to send out detachments. For instance, when I deployed detachments in Upper Silesia, they were relatively safe because they kept to the areas near fortified places, as I previously advised. This closeness to strongholds provided them with a safe haven if threatened by the enemy.

Officers tasked with leading detachments should be men of sound judgment and strong resolve. Although they receive general orders from their commanding officer, they must be prepared to independently decide when to advance or retreat, based on their specific situation. If the enemy's force is too powerful, they should pull back strategically. Conversely, if they have the upper hand, they must recognize this advantage and seize the moment. Such decisions require an officer to be flexible and responsive to changing circumstances, knowing that each choice could turn the tide of battle.

If the enemy approaches by night, these officers may sometimes find it prudent to feign a retreat. In some cases, while the enemy believes they're in retreat, the detachment can suddenly regroup and launch a surprise attack, catching the enemy off guard. This tactic can be effective in breaking the enemy's formation and morale. Light troops, however, need not be a concern in these maneuvers.

The primary duty of an officer in command of a detachment is to ensure his own safety and that of his men. Once this is achieved, he can turn his focus to planning and executing attacks against the enemy. Keeping his adversary on high alert by frequently taking the offensive will ensure the enemy is unable to rest. If this officer can succeed in two or three such instances, the enemy will eventually be forced onto the defensive, a position that will grant his forces an advantage.

If these detachments are close to the main army, they should establish communication lines using either a nearby town or forest as a conduit. This connection is crucial for relaying information, coordinating movements, and ensuring that both the main force and the detachment can offer support if either comes under attack. Maintaining such a link enhances the detachment's effectiveness, keeping it as an extension of the main force rather than an isolated unit vulnerable to enemy strikes.

In a defensive war, we often find ourselves needing to make detachments. Generals with limited experience tend to worry about preserving everything, while a skilled and daring leader focuses only on the main objective, aiming to strike a significant blow. Such a leader accepts smaller setbacks if they help prevent a larger disaster.

The enemy's army should be our primary focus. We must work to uncover their plans and counter them with as much force as possible. In 1745, we chose to leave Upper Silesia exposed to Hungarian raids so that we could better interfere with the plans of Prince Charles of Lorraine. We refrained from making any detachments until after we defeated his army. Once that victory was secured, General Nassau cleared Upper Silesia of the Hungarians in just fifteen days.

Some generals have a habit of making detachments before launching an attack, intending for these forces to strike the enemy from the rear during the battle. However, this approach is risky because the detachments often lose their way and end up arriving either too soon or too late. For example, when Charles XII sent out a detachment on the night before the Battle of Poltava, they got lost, which contributed to the army's defeat. Similarly, Prince Eugene's plan to surprise

Cremona failed when the Prince of Vaudemont's detachment arrived too late to attack the Po Gate as planned.

Detachments should never be made on the day of battle unless it's done with careful strategy, like Turenne's maneuver near Colmar. There, he presented his first line to the army of Elector Frederick William while his second line moved through narrow passes to strike the enemy's flank, leading to their rout. Another example comes from Marshal de Luxembourg at the Battle of Fleurus in 1690, where he hid a group of infantry in tall corn on Prince Waldeck's flank, and this tactic won him the battle.

Only after a victory, and never before, can troops be detached to protect supply convoys. Even then, they should not move farther than half a league from the main army.

In conclusion, detachments that weaken an army by half or even by a third are extremely dangerous and should be firmly avoided.

ARTICLE X

OF THE TRICKS AND STRATAGEMS OF WAR

In war, the skill of a fox can sometimes be just as essential as the strength of a lion, because cleverness and subtlety may accomplish what sheer power cannot. Since brute force can, at times, be countered by equal force, or even bested by clever strategies, we must be thoroughly skilled in both methods. This knowledge enables us to use either force or cunning as the situation demands, ensuring we can adapt and succeed in the face of different challenges.

I won't attempt to recount the countless strategies that have been used in warfare, as they all share a common goal: to mislead and exhaust the enemy by making him move or prepare unnecessarily. When we effectively conceal our true intentions, we keep our enemy guessing, preventing him from countering our actual plans and positioning our forces to advantage. Therefore, it is vital to lead the enemy to believe that we are planning moves that we have no intention of executing. In doing so, we force him to respond to phantom threats, weakening his position and creating opportunities for us to strike effectively.

When we are gathering troops, we often march them

in various directions, creating confusion to keep the enemy uncertain about where we truly plan to assemble. By keeping our destination ambiguous, we prevent the enemy from reinforcing his defenses in the area we actually aim to attack. In regions where there are fortresses or strongholds, we choose a campsite that appears to threaten multiple locations at once. By doing so, the enemy may feel compelled to divide his forces, reinforcing several of these areas at the same time. This division weakens his main body of troops, making it easier for us to attack when the right moment arises. However, if he chooses to focus on just one location, this also serves us well, as we can then concentrate our efforts on laying siege to whichever fortress appears most vulnerable.

If our goal is to cross a river or seize a position of particular importance, we begin by withdrawing to a considerable distance from both the crossing point and the position we intend to capture. This maneuver lures the enemy away from our actual target, leading him to believe that he no longer needs to guard it closely. Then, when our troops are fully prepared, and our movements remain hidden, we return quickly to the pre-determined location, seizing control of it before the enemy can reposition.

When we desire a battle, but the enemy shows a clear reluctance to engage, we employ tactics to make him believe we are fearful of his strength. For instance, we may spread rumors that our own forces are weak, diminished, or in disarray. This tactic was effectively used before the Battle of Hohenfriedberg, when I ordered roads to be repaired as though I planned to retreat to Breslau in four columns, at the approach of Prince Charles. His overconfidence worked in our favor, as he pursued us onto the plain, and we were able to achieve victory.

At times, we even shrink the size of our camp to give the appearance of having a smaller force. By keeping detachments out in the open, we make the enemy believe they're of greater importance than they truly are. Such tactics lead him to underestimate us, causing him to overlook chances to attack when they arise. For example, during the 1745 campaign, if my goal had been to take Königgrätz and Pardubice, I would have needed only two marches across the Glatz region toward Moravia. This would almost certainly have alarmed Prince Charles, prompting him to rush to protect the areas from which he drew his supplies after leaving Bohemia, thus leaving other positions vulnerable. By merely threatening locations linked to his supply routes or those connected with the capital, we can create a sense of vulnerability and sow doubt within the enemy ranks.

If we have no intention of engaging in battle, we make an effort to present ourselves as a formidable and confident force, spreading rumors of our strength and readiness. Austria has mastered this approach, turning it into a refined art form where they appear stronger than they are, intimidating their opponents with mere appearances.

By keeping up a bold and determined front, we project the image that we are eager for battle and that we have a daring plan in place. Such a display encourages rumors that we are about to launch a bold, risky maneuver, which often makes the enemy hesitant, fearing the consequences of an engagement. By leading him to believe we have some bold or daring plan in mind, we keep the enemy on edge, making him wary and defensive. Often, this bold appearance alone is enough to make him stay on the defensive, avoiding any confrontation altogether, and ensuring our troops maintain their advantage.

In a defensive war, one of the most important skills is choosing strong positions and holding them until the very last moment. When forced to retreat, the second line of defense should be the first to begin moving back, followed gradually by the first line. With natural barriers, like defiles, in front of you, the enemy will find it difficult to take advantage of your retreat, keeping your forces protected as they withdraw.

Even during the retreat, it is crucial to select positions that are angled and unclear, making it hard for the enemy to understand your intentions. The more the enemy tries to interpret your movements, the more uncertain he will become, while you indirectly achieve your desired objective without giving away your true strategy.

One effective tactic in warfare is to present a broad front, creating an illusion of a large-scale engagement. If the enemy mistakes this feint for an actual attack, he will be caught off guard and will likely suffer defeat. Through these deceptive maneuvers, you can prompt the enemy to send out detachments, taking advantage of his divided forces to strike with precision.

One of the best stratagems is to lull the enemy into a false sense of security, particularly as winter approaches and troops prepare to disperse and settle into winter quarters. By retreating under the guise of ending the campaign season, you can prepare to reassemble your forces quickly and catch the enemy off guard. To do this effectively, troops should be distributed in a way that allows for swift regrouping, enabling a surprise advance on the enemy's quarters. If successful, this strategy can undo the setbacks of an entire campaign within a matter of weeks.

A careful study of Turenne's last two campaigns

provides an excellent example of such tactics; they are considered masterpieces of stratagem from this era. Our ancestors' techniques for warfare have largely been relegated to light troops, who still use ambushes and feigned retreats to draw the enemy into narrow spaces where they can be surrounded and defeated. However, generals today rarely fall for such basic traps, having become wise to these older tricks. Yet even skilled leaders can be vulnerable to betrayal; for instance, Charles XII was misled at Poltava due to the treachery of a Cossack chief, and Peter I faced a similar fate on the Pruth due to the failure of a local prince who could not provide the promised supplies.

As for the methods of conducting warfare through parties and detachments, these are detailed extensively in my *Military Regulation*. Anyone who wishes to refresh their memory on these tactics should refer to that document, as there is little else I need to add on this subject here.

To understand how to compel the enemy to make detachments, we need only examine the brilliant campaign of 1690, led by Marshal de Luxembourg against the King of England. This campaign, culminating in the Battle of Neerwinden, is a prime example of how to keep the enemy divided and vulnerable through strategic maneuvers.

ARTICLE XI

OF SPIES, HOW THEY ARE TO BE EMPLOYED ON EVERY OCCASION, AND IN WHAT MANNER WE ARE TO LEARN INTELLIGENCE OF THE ENEMY.

If we could know the enemy's intentions ahead of time, we would always have an upper hand, even with a smaller force. This advantage is highly sought by generals but rarely obtained. The use of spies is essential in this regard, and they fall into several categories: 1) ordinary individuals who volunteer for this work;

2) double agents; 3) high-value spies with access to important information; and 4) those forced into this unpleasant line of duty.

The first type, ordinary individuals like peasants, artisans, priests, and others who enter the enemy's camp, can only be used to locate where the enemy is stationed. Their reports, however, are often vague or contradictory, which can increase our uncertainty rather than reduce it.

The intelligence gathered from deserters is usually no more reliable. A soldier may know what's happening within his own regiment but is unlikely to have insight into broader plans. As for hussars, who are frequently dispatched ahead and spend much time away from the main army, they may not even know where the army is camped. Despite these limitations, we still commit all reports to writing, as that is the only way to derive any potential benefit from them.

Double agents, on the other hand, are spies used to feed false information to the enemy. For example, an Italian at Schmiedeberg acted as a spy for the Austrians. When we told him that we intended to withdraw to Breslau if the enemy approached, he hurried to report this to Prince Charles of Lorraine, who came close to being deceived by this misinformation.

High-ranking spies, or those with direct access to critical intelligence, are invaluable assets. The postmaster at Versailles, for instance, worked secretly for Prince Eugene. This unfortunate man would open letters and orders sent from the court to the generals, copying their contents and forwarding them to Prince Eugene, who often received these messages even before the French commanders did. Similarly, Luxembourg managed to win the loyalty of a secretary to the King of England, who then informed Luxembourg of sensitive information. The king discovered this betrayal, turning it to his advantage. He forced the traitor to write to Luxembourg with a report that the allied army would go out the next day on a major foraging mission. This nearly led to the French being ambushed at Steenkerque, and they would have been destroyed if not for their exceptional defense.

Securing such spies in a war against Austria, however, would be highly challenging. This isn't because Austrians are less susceptible to bribery, but because their army is surrounded by a swarm of light troops who inspect all who pass through their lines thoroughly. This challenge led me to consider persuading some of their hussar officers to join our side, allowing us to establish a line of communication in the following way: when hussars engage in skirmishes, they sometimes agree to a brief truce. Such occasions could provide an opportunity to exchange messages discreetly.

In cases where we want to gather intelligence on the enemy or mislead him about our circumstances, we can send a loyal soldier from our camp to theirs to spread whatever information we want them to believe. This soldier might carry handbills encouraging desertion, return by a roundabout route, and bring back any information he can gather.

There is another, harsher way to gather intelligence when less severe measures fail, though I admit it is a cruel method. We identify a wealthy citizen with a large family and considerable property. Then, we assign him a person fluent in the enemy's language, disguised as his servant. This "servant" accompanies him to the enemy's camp under the pretense that the citizen is there to complain of injustices he has suffered. To ensure his cooperation, we threaten that if he does not return within a set time, bringing his servant with him, we will burn his house and harm his family. I had to resort to this tactic once, and it worked as I hoped.

Finally, it's worth noting that when paying spies, we must be generous, even to the point of extravagance. A person who risks his life to provide valuable information deserves to be well- compensated for his courage.

ARTICLE XII

OF CERTAIN MARKS, BY WHICH THE INTENTIONS OF THE ENEMY ARE TO BE DISCOVERED.

Understanding where the enemy has established his main depot for provisions is one of the most reliable ways to anticipate his intentions before the campaign begins. For instance, if the Austrians set up their supply depots at Olmütz, it's almost certain they plan to launch an attack on Upper Silesia. If they place them in Königgrätz, it's a strong indication that the region around Schweidnitz may be targeted. Likewise, when the Saxons aimed to invade the Electorate's border, the locations of their supply depots—Zittau, Görlitz, and Guben—revealed their intended path, as these towns lie along the route to Crossen.

Therefore, the primary objective in gathering intelligence should be identifying where the enemy has decided to place their supply depots and understanding the positions in which they are established. The French, for example, used a cunning tactic by setting up supply depots on both the Meuse and the Scheldt rivers to obscure their true plans, giving them flexibility and creating uncertainty for their adversaries.

The Austrians, on the other hand, often give away their movements through certain customs. For example, when they are preparing to march, they usually cook early in the morning on the day of departure. If significant smoke is observed in their camp around five or six in the morning, it's a reliable sign that they intend to break camp and move out that day.

Moreover, when the Austrians are preparing for battle, they tend to recall all of their strong detachments of light troops, consolidating their forces in preparation for the fight. If this is noticed, it is a clear signal to stay vigilant and prepare for immediate engagement.

If you are attacking a position defended by Hungarian troops and find it highly resistant to your assault, this may indicate that the main Austrian army is nearby, ready to provide reinforcement. Similarly, if the enemy's light troops maneuver to place themselves between your main army and one of your detached forces, it's a strong indication that the enemy has targeted that detachment, and you should make the necessary preparations to counter this move.

If you consistently face the same general on the opposing side, his tactics and intentions will eventually become apparent. Over time, his strategies and habitual methods will grow familiar, allowing you to anticipate his actions more easily.

After carefully evaluating the terrain of the war theater, the current condition of your army, the security of your supply depots, the strength of your fortified positions, and the potential strategies the enemy might use to capture these resources, it's essential to consider the risks posed by the enemy's light troops. These troops may position themselves along your flanks, rear, or other vulnerable spots or be deployed for diversionary tactics. Taking all these elements into account, you can reasonably assume that an intelligent enemy will pursue an operation that promises to disrupt you in the most damaging way. At the very least, this will likely be his intent, and you must focus all your efforts on countering it to protect your position effectively.

OF OUR OWN COUNTRY, AND THAT WHICH IS EITHER NEUTRAL OR HOSTILE; OF THE VARIETY OF RELIGIONS, AND OF THE DIFFERENT CONDUCT WHICH SUCH CIRCUMSTANCES REQUIRE.

War can be conducted in one of three types of territories: our own lands, those belonging to neutral powers, or the land of the enemy. If my sole aim were glory, I would only wage war within my own country, due to the numerous advantages it provides. Every inhabitant becomes a potential informant, making it nearly impossible for the enemy to move undetected.

In our own country, we can safely send out large detachments that can perform any military maneuver with confidence. When the enemy gains an advantage, the local population often takes up arms to resist, just as they did after the Battle of Fehrbellin. At that time, Elector Frederick William saw more Swedes fall to the hands of the peasants than on the battlefield itself. Similarly, after the Battle of Hohenfriedberg, I saw the mountaineers in Silesia capturing and delivering fleeing Austrians to us in large numbers.

When war takes place in a neutral country, both sides have an equal footing, and the main focus shifts to winning the favor and trust of the local population. Achieving this requires strict discipline among the troops, banning any form of looting or theft, and enforcing such rules with severe penalties. It might also help to suggest that the enemy has harmful intentions toward the country, thereby turning the locals against them.

If the country is Protestant, we can pose as protectors of the Lutheran faith, stirring religious fervor among the lower classes, who are often susceptible to our persuasive tactics. In a Catholic country, we promote tolerance and moderation, blaming religious animosities on the priests, who we claim are responsible for much of the existing tensions between different groups. Despite their conflicts, people of different sects often agree on core tenets of faith, which we can use to our advantage.

The size of any detachment we send out must reflect the trustworthiness of the local populace. In our own country, we can take almost any risk, knowing we have widespread support. In a neutral country, however, more caution is required, at least until we're certain that the majority of the population harbors no hostility. Once their trust is secured, detachments can be dispatched with more confidence.

In a thoroughly hostile country, such as Bohemia or Moravia, we must take no risks, sending out no detachments for the reasons previously discussed, as the inhabitants cannot be trusted beyond what we can directly observe. Here, most light troops are best employed to guard convoys, as it's unrealistic to expect any positive sentiment from the population. The Hussites around

Königgrätz are the only ones who might offer assistance. Those of influence may appear friendly but are traitorous at heart; nor are the priests or local magistrates any more reliable. With their interests tied to Austria, whose objectives do not entirely align with ours, we should neither trust nor rely on them in any capacity.

Our remaining option in such places is to appeal to religious zeal, stirring up passion for religious liberty and subtly suggesting to the population that their priests and noble leaders keep them under oppressive rule. This, one might say, is a matter of invoking powerful forces to serve our interests.

Since I recorded these thoughts, the Empress-Queen has significantly raised taxes in Bohemia and Moravia. This change could be used to gain the goodwill of the people, especially if we imply that they would be treated more favorably should we take control of the region.

ARTICLE XIV

OF EVERY KIND OF MARCH, WHICH IT CAN BE NECESSARYFOR AN ARMY TO MAKE.

An army moves with specific purposes in mind: advancing into enemy territory, securing a strategic campsite, joining with reinforcements, preparing for battle, or retreating before the enemy. Once the camp is well-fortified, the next priority is to scout the surrounding area and all roads leading into and out of the camp. This reconnaissance allows for precise planning in response to various scenarios.

To achieve this, large detachments are sent out under various pretexts, accompanied by engineers and quartermasters who examine every location that could potentially be occupied by troops. Their job is to analyze the terrain and survey the roads that the army might need to use. Following them are several chasseurs, whose task is to study these roads in detail so they can effectively guide the columns should the general decide to march along those routes.

Upon returning, these officers provide a thorough

report on the camp's location, the roads leading to it, the characteristics of the land, and the nearby woods, mountains, and rivers. With this information in hand, the general is equipped to make informed decisions. When the camp isn't too close to the enemy, a specific marching order can be implemented as follows:

Imagine that the camp can be accessed by four different routes. The advance guard, which consists of six battalions of grenadiers, one infantry regiment, two dragoon regiments (each with five squadrons), and two hussar regiments under the command of Mr.

N. N., will depart at eight o'clock this evening. All of the army's encampments will follow this advance guard, which will carry only its tents and leave the heavier baggage with the main army.

These troops will march four leagues ahead, securing any important features they encounter—such as defiles, rivers, hills, towns, or villages—until the main army arrives. Once the main army reaches them, the advance guard will then enter the camp that has already been designated.

The following morning, the main army, arranged in four columns, will advance behind the lead of the advance guard. Soldiers stationed as guards in villages along the route will rejoin their respective regiments. The right-wing cavalry, split into two lines and marching on the right, will form the first column. The infantry of the right wing, also in two lines and marching by the right, will create the second column. The infantry of the left wing, filing by the right as well, will establish the third column. Finally, the left-wing cavalry, likewise filing by the right, will constitute the fourth column.

The regiments N. N. of the second line, along with three hussar regiments under General N. N., will escort the baggage, which will follow behind the two infantry columns. Four aides-de-camp will supervise this escort to ensure that the carriages proceed in a well-ordered line with minimal gaps between them.

If the rear guard general requires additional support, he must immediately alert the commander in chief. The chasseurs who initially scouted the roads will guide the four columns to ensure they follow the intended paths accurately.

In advance of each column, a team of carpenters will travel with wagons carrying beams, joists, and planks to construct bridges over smaller rivers as necessary. Column leaders must ensure that each column progresses at an even pace, without moving ahead of one another, and with controlled spacing. Division officers need to monitor their distances carefully, maintaining cohesion.

When crossing a defile, the heads of each column should march slowly or pause intermittently to allow the rear to maintain alignment. This steady pace ensures the entire march remains well-coordinated.

The march continues with this order in mind. When the army encounters mountains, forests, or defiles, the columns should split, allowing the infantry to lead, followed by the cavalry, which will close the march and provide additional protection from behind.

If a plain lies at the center of the area, it should be designated for the cavalry, while the infantry, organized into columns at both ends, should move through the woods. However, this setup applies only when the march is taking place at a safe distance from the enemy. When closer to the enemy, it's sufficient to place a few battalions of grenadiers at the head of each cavalry column to help maintain the battle order.

The most reliable way to ensure a reinforcement reaches us safely is to march along a challenging road to meet it, simultaneously distancing ourselves from the enemy to avoid any confrontation. The advantage gained from the arrival of reinforcements will soon allow us to retake any ground temporarily conceded to the enemy.

When circumstances require marching parallel to the enemy, it should be conducted in two lines, either to the right or left, with each line forming a column and accompanied by an advance guard at the front. The same principles I previously outlined can also be applied here.

All of our marches from Frankenberg to Hohen-friedberg were organized in this manner, consistently moving to the right. I favor these arrangements over others because the army can be easily organized into battle formation by a single movement to the right or left, which is the quickest way to assemble them. This method would always be my preference when engaging the enemy if I had the option, even though I lost the benefit of it at Sohr and Hohenfriedberg. In this style of march, it is essential to ensure that the flank never exposes itself to the enemy.

When the enemy begins a march indicating preparations for battle, it is important to offload all heavy baggage and send it with an escort to the nearest town for safekeeping. The advance guard should then be formed and sent forward to a distance of roughly half a league.

When marching directly toward the enemy, special care must be taken to prevent columns from advancing too far ahead of one another. As they approach the battlefield, the columns should spread out in such a way that the troops occupy precisely the amount of ground they will need in battle formation. This task is challenging, as some battalions often find themselves too crowded, while others end up with too much space.

Marching in lines presents no particular disadvantage, which is why I have always preferred it.

When a battle is expected during the march, extreme caution is required. The general must remain vigilant, surveying the terrain cautiously from one vantage point to another without overexposing himself, in order to develop a clear understanding of different possible positions should the enemy attempt an attack.

Church steeples and elevated areas should be used to gain a view of the terrain, and any paths leading to these vantage points should be cleared by light troops dispatched from the advance guard.

Retreats are typically organized as follows: one or two days before departure, the heavy baggage is assembled and sent off under a strong escort.

The number of columns in a march should be carefully chosen based on how many usable roads are available and, equally importantly, on the nature of the terrain. In open plains, where space is abundant, it is most effective to have the cavalry lead the advance guard, as their mobility and speed make them well- suited for this task. However, if the landscape is more varied, with mixed fields, woods, and potential obstacles, it becomes safer to assign the advance guard duties to the infantry, as they can adapt more readily to varied terrain. When marching in open country, it's typical for the army to be organized into four columns.

In such an arrangement, the right wing's second line

of infantry, filing by the right and followed by the cavalry of the same wing, will form the fourth column. Similarly, the first line of the right- wing infantry will also file by its right, followed by its cavalry, forming the third column. On the left wing, the second line of infantry, accompanied by its corresponding cavalry, will make up the second column. Finally, the infantry of the left wing's first line, followed by its cavalry, will compose the first column.

With this formation, the entire rear guard is made up of the cavalry, which provides flexibility and, if necessary, can be reinforced by hussars for added security. The rear guard plays a vital role in ensuring the protection of slower-moving troops and equipment, giving the main body of the army time to maneuver as needed.

During a retreat that requires crossing a defile, it's critical for the infantry to secure the passage the evening before departure. By positioning themselves strategically, they shield the rest of the troops, ensuring that the defile remains open and accessible. In this way, if any resistance or unexpected challenges arise, the infantry can provide cover, allowing the rest of the army to move through safely.

If circumstances require the army to move in only two columns, this will alter the arrangement somewhat. In such a case, the cavalry of the right wing will file to the left, with the second line moving first and taking the lead in the second column. Following this, the second line of infantry will fall into place, with the first line of infantry filing behind them to complete the formation. On the left wing, the second line of cavalry will also file by the left, moving first and taking the lead of the first column. This first column is then completed by the infantry of the left wing, with the second line moving first, followed by the first line.

The rear guard in this arrangement is strengthened by six battalions from the rear of the first line, accompanied by ten squadrons of hussars. These battalions and squadrons position themselves in a two-line formation at the front of the defile, adopting a checkerboard pattern to secure the area as the army moves through. While the main force passes through the defile, these rear guard troops use their positioning to provide cover fire, protecting those troops still on the other side.

Once the army has fully crossed, the advance guard's first line moves into the defile, passing through openings in the second line. After this first line is through, the second line follows under the cover of the rear guard, which remains stationed on the opposite side to maintain protection until the last units have safely passed.

One of the most challenging maneuvers is to cross a river while in retreat, especially when the enemy is close. An excellent example of this complex operation is our retreat across the Elbe at Kolin in 1744, where careful planning and disciplined execution enabled a successful crossing under pressure.

However, suitable towns or strongholds are not always nearby to support such maneuvers. In cases where two bridges are the only available crossing points, a large entrenchment should be constructed to secure both bridges, with small openings left at the heads of each bridge. Once this entrenchment is in place, several artillery pieces and a designated number of troops should be positioned on the far bank of the river. This opposite bank should have a moderate slope—steep enough to provide a height advantage but gentle enough to permit maneuvering. This elevated position enables these troops to control the crossing area, keeping enemy forces at bay.

With the entrenchment manned by infantry, the main force can proceed with the crossing, beginning with the infantry. The cavalry remains behind, forming a checkerboard arrangement within the entrenchment to act as the rear guard, providing cover for the crossing. Once the majority of the army has crossed, the infantry positioned at the heads of the bridges can take up positions to cover the last stages of the withdrawal.

If the enemy attempts a pursuit, they will be met by concentrated fire from troops positioned at both bridgeheads as well as from the forces stationed across the river. This setup provides a layered defense that can significantly hinder the enemy's advance.

When the entrenchment's infantry has crossed the river, the bridge itself should be dismantled or destroyed, preventing the enemy from following. Those troops who had been stationed at the bridgeheads can then cross by boat, shielded by supporting troops on the far side who are ready to advance and assist if needed.

Once the pontoons are loaded onto their carriages, the remaining troops can begin their movement, completing the withdrawal.

At the angles of the entrenchment, fougasses (explosive traps) can be strategically placed. The last grenadiers to cross the river will ignite these fougasses to disrupt any pursuing forces, giving the army time to establish a safe distance.

ARTICLE XV

ON THE PRECAUTIONS NECESSARY TO BE TAKEN IN A RETREAT AGAINST HUSSARS AND PANDOURS.

Hussars and pandours may seem terrifying to those who aren't familiar with their methods, but their courage is often superficial. They're brave only when they're driven by the promise of loot or when they can harass others without risking their own safety. Their tactics mainly involve two types of aggression: one directed at convoys and baggage trains, where they seek easy plunder, and the other aimed at troops forced into retreat, where they attempt to annoy and hinder the soldiers' withdrawal.

While our regular troops have little to genuinely fear from these forces, the skirmishing methods of the hussars and pandours can delay our marches. Their attacks are inconvenient, especially since we inevitably lose some men—often at critical moments. For this reason, I will explain the most effective way I know to handle these opponents.

When retreating through open plains, we can typically drive off the hussars with a few well-placed cannon shots, while the pandours can be kept at bay with our dragoons and hussars, who inspire significant fear in them. However, the most challenging retreats occur when our path takes us through forests, narrow passes, or mountainous terrain, as these areas give pandours ample opportunity to inflict damage. In such situations, it is almost unavoidable that we will suffer some losses.

In these difficult environments, the heights should first be secured by our advance guard, positioned with their front facing the enemy. At the same time, we should detach troops to the flanks of the marching column, allowing them to traverse the heights and woods alongside the main body. Additional squadrons should be kept ready to engage wherever the ground allows.

In these scenarios, it is crucial to maintain steady movement without halting, as a stop would only expose some of our men unnecessarily, leading to preventable casualties. The pandours typically lie flat as they fire, keeping themselves well hidden, and when our army's advance forces the rear guard and small detached units to abandon their positions, the pandours quickly occupy these vacated spots. From these concealed positions, often behind trees or on higher ground, they pick off retreating soldiers with relative safety.

Neither musket fire nor cannon loaded with cartridges can effectively target them, as they remain dispersed and hidden behind terrain features like hills and trees.

I faced two retreats under these conditions in 1745: the first through the valley of Liebenthal en route to Staudenitz and the second from Trautenau to Schatzlar. Despite every possible precaution, we lost sixty men killed and wounded in the first retreat and over two hundred in the second.

In cases where we must retreat along difficult paths, our marches should be kept very short, allowing us to stay vigilant and prepared. No march should exceed two leagues, or roughly one German mile. This measured pace reduces strain on the troops, enabling us to respond more effectively to any pandour attacks. If the pandours are careless enough to take refuge in a wood, we sometimes have the advantage of turning their position, forcing them to either flee or face us directly.

OF THE METHOD IN WHICH THE LIGHT PRUSSIAN TROOPS CONDUCT THEMSELVES WHEN ENGAGED WITH THE HUSSARS AND PANDOURS.

When we aim to dislodge enemy light troops from a position, our approach is to launch a swift and forceful attack. Given that these light troops tend to scatter in their fighting style, they are poorly equipped to withstand a direct assault from our disciplined forces, who are trained to engage with full commitment and without hesitation.

To execute this plan, we first detach a few units to secure the flanks of the main force advancing against the light troops. With the flanks protected, we then attack with vigor, ensuring a high chance that the enemy will break and flee.

Our dragoons and hussars, advancing in tightly formed ranks with swords drawn, engage these light troops directly. This type of close combat is something light troops are generally unprepared for and incapable of enduring. In every instance, this approach has proven effective, allowing us to drive them off without concern for any numerical advantage they might possess.

BY WHAT MOVEMENTS ON OUR SIDE THE ENEMY MAY ALSO BE OBLIGED TO MOVE.

It is a grave mistake to think that merely moving an army will compel the enemy to respond by moving as well. Forcing the enemy into action isn't achieved simply by movement; it requires a deliberate and calculated approach in how that movement is executed. An intelligent adversary won't be easily swayed by superficial maneuvers you may employ. Instead, you must take up strategically significant positions that will compel the enemy to think deeply about his options and eventually force him to abandon his own camp.

To execute this effectively, you need a thorough understanding of the terrain, the capabilities of the opposing general, the locations of his supply depots, the towns that provide him with resources, and the areas from which he gathers forage. Only after carefully analyzing these factors can a solid plan be formulated. A general who employs a creative and determined approach to unsettle his enemy will, in time, earn the distinction of challenging his opponent in both skill and reputation.

At the onset of a campaign, the general who promptly gathers his forces, advances to seize a town or occupies a key position will immediately set the pace, forcing his opponent into a reactive, defensive posture. However, there should always be sound strategic reasons behind any attempt to force the enemy to move during a campaign. This may include securing a nearby town close to his encampment, driving him into desolate territory where sustaining his forces becomes difficult, or creating conditions that favor a decisive engagement. With such clear objectives in mind, you begin to develop a plan that considers both the risks and benefits of each maneuver.

It is vital that the marches you undertake and the camps you occupy do not create greater challenges for you than for the enemy. For example, drawing too far away from your depot may expose it to attack by enemy light troops, especially if it is inadequately fortified. Similarly, taking up a position that disconnects you from supply lines or communications with your own country could lead to shortages that force a retreat.

After carefully evaluating these considerations and calculating the potential actions of the enemy, you can then determine your approach. This may include setting up camp on one of the enemy's flanks, moving closer to the regions that provide his sustenance, cutting off his access to his capital, threatening his supply depots, or choosing a position that disrupts his access to essential provisions.

A concrete example of such a strategy, well-known to many of my officers, occurred when I planned to force Prince Charles of Lorraine to abandon Königgrätz and Pardubitz in 1745.

Upon leaving the camp at Dubletz, our route should have taken us leftward, skirting the Glatz region and advancing near Hohenmauth. This maneuver would have pressured the Austrians, who relied on supply depots in Teutschbrod and mostly drew their provisions from Moravia, to move to Landscron, effectively conceding Königgrätz and Pardubitz to us. The Saxons, being cut off from their homeland, would have been forced to leave the Austrians and return to defend their own territory.

I ultimately refrained from executing this maneuver because, even if I had secured Königgrätz, it would have been of limited benefit. I would still have needed to send detachments to support Prince of Anhalt if the Saxons decided to return home. Additionally, the supply depots at Glatz could not sustain my entire army for the length of the campaign, rendering such a position unsustainable.

Creating diversions by dispatching troops to separate areas can also pressure the enemy into breaking camp. Generally, any unexpected operation that catches the enemy off-guard has the potential to disrupt his plans, forcing him to abandon his current position. Such operations include crossing mountains that the enemy believes to be impassable or fording rivers without his knowledge.

The campaign of Prince Eugene in 1701 provides valuable insight into these tactics. The disarray of the French army when Prince Charles of Lorraine unexpectedly crossed the Rhine serves as a well-known example of how such maneuvers can unsettle an enemy force.

In conclusion, the success of these operations lies in ensuring that the execution aligns with the intent. As long as the general's plans are carefully crafted and based on solid strategic principles, he will be able to dictate terms to the enemy, forcing him to remain on the defensive. By maintaining this strategic advantage, the general keeps control of the campaign, always a step ahead of his adversary.

ARTICLE XVIII

OF THE CROSSING OF RIVERS

When the enemy remains on the opposite side of a river that we aim to cross, brute force alone is futile; instead, strategic deception becomes essential. To understand how to execute a successful river crossing, we need only examine Caesar's crossing of the Rhine, Prince Eugene's crossing of the Po, or Prince Charles of Lorraine's crossing of the Rhine. These generals used detachments to mislead the enemy, obscuring the actual crossing point. They prepared bridges in locations where they had no intention of crossing, thus misleading the enemy, while the main body of the army marched under cover of night to a significant distance away, allowing them time to cross the river before the enemy forces could organize a defense.

Rivers are generally crossed at points where there are small islands, as these natural features provide valuable support for establishing a foothold. It is also preferable to encounter woods or other natural obstructions on the opposite bank, which hinder the enemy from launching an immediate counterattack, giving us time to organize our troops once across.

Such operations demand meticulous planning and

vigilance. Boats, pontoons, and all other necessary equipment must be in place by the designated time, with each boatman thoroughly briefed on the typical demands of night operations. Once every component is in order, the troops proceed to cross and secure a position on the opposite bank.

In any river-crossing operation, it is crucial to fortify both bridgeheads, placing ample troops to hold these positions. Nearby islands should be fortified to reinforce the bridgehead defenses and prevent the enemy from seizing or damaging the bridge during the crossing.

For narrower rivers, it is advantageous to select crossing points where the river creates natural angles or bends, with slightly elevated banks that provide a vantage over the opposite side. At such locations, we position as many cannons as the terrain permits, along with a proportional number of troops, to cover the construction of bridges. As the angle creates a narrower stretch of land, we advance carefully and gain ground gradually as the troops cross.

If fords are available, the approach should be smoothed to facilitate the cavalry's crossing, ensuring an effective and coordinated river passage.

ARTICLE XIX

OF THE MANNER IN WHICH THE PASSAGE OF RIVERS IS TO BE DEFENDED.

Defending the crossing of a river, especially when the area to be covered is vast, is one of the most difficult tasks in warfare, if not altogether impractical. Successfully defending a river crossing requires specific conditions. The section of the river to be defended should not exceed eight German miles in width, as a broader front would be impossible to cover effectively. Additionally, two or three well-placed redoubts must be established along the riverbank within this range, and there should be no fords available elsewhere that might allow the enemy to bypass these defenses and cross unimpeded.

Assuming these conditions are met, adequate time is crucial to properly prepare for the enemy's crossing attempts. The preparations should follow a precise defensive strategy to cover all vulnerabilities.

To begin, gather all available boats, barges, and any other watercraft from the river and relocate them to the redoubt areas. This prevents the enemy from using these vessels to cross the river or otherwise aid in their approach. Next, conduct a thorough reconnaissance of both riverbanks to identify and obstruct any potential crossing points. Every possible location where the enemy might find cover during an attempted crossing must be given special attention, as these areas can offer them protection from our defensive positions.

Once the crossing points are identified, preparations for defense must consider the terrain's specifics. Roads wide enough to support multiple columns should be constructed along the entire defensive front, ensuring that troops can move rapidly without congestion. These roads allow our forces to reposition and reinforce different areas of the defense line without delay, maintaining a flexible but robust defense.

With the defenses in place, the main army should camp at the center of the defensive line, reducing the distance to either end to just four miles, allowing quick access to all points of defense. From this central position, form sixteen mobile detachments commanded by the most diligent and alert officers among the dragoons and hussars. These officers should be handpicked for their intelligence and adaptability. Split the detachments equally: eight assigned to cover the right flank of the defense line and the remaining eight to guard the left flank, each group under the command of a capable general officer.

These detachments serve dual roles. They constantly monitor the enemy's movements, detecting any signs of an attempted crossing, and report any significant activity or shifts in the enemy's positions. During the daytime, guard posts are strategically positioned along the riverbanks to observe any preparations the enemy might be undertaking. At night, patrols should be sent out every fifteen minutes, advancing to the river's edge and remaining there until they have a clear view of the enemy's bridge-building efforts or detect the leading edge of an attempted crossing.

The generals overseeing these detachments, along with the officers in command of the redoubts, must send reports to the commander in chief four times per day. To expedite communication, a relay of fresh horses should be placed between the front lines and the main army to ensure messages reach the commander as swiftly as possible, giving him immediate awareness of any enemy activity at the river. The general must be prepared to respond to a breach in defenses at a moment's notice; for this reason, his baggage should be sent ahead to avoid any delay in his movements.

Each segment of the defensive line should have specific, pre- planned countermeasures ready for activation when the enemy's crossing attempt begins. The commander in chief assigns experienced generals to manage the defense at key points along the river. Upon receiving notice of the enemy's attempt to cross, the army should advance swiftly, with the infantry leading the columns, as it is presumed that the enemy will immediately begin entrenching once they establish a foothold on the other side. Speed and decisiveness are crucial upon arrival at the crossing point; a rapid, forceful attack is the best chance of successfully repelling the enemy and preventing them from establishing a secure position.

Defending the crossing of smaller rivers, though seemingly easier, presents its own set of challenges, often making such defenses even more difficult. If the river contains fords, every effort should be made to render them impassable by blocking them with felled trees or other debris to prevent enemy cavalry from advancing. However, if the enemy's bank is elevated above ours, resistance becomes nearly futile, as they will have the advantage of height for both cover and attack.

Regarding the surprise capture of towns, a successful surprise relies on several favorable conditions. A town susceptible to surprise is often poorly guarded and lacks strong fortifications. If the town's ditches are water-filled, a surprise attack can only succeed during winter, when a hard frost makes the water a negligible obstacle.

Surprises can be conducted by an entire army, as demonstrated by the capture of Prague in 1741. Alternatively, they may result from a prolonged blockade that leads the defenders to a false sense of security, as in Prince Leopold of Anhalt's capture of Glogau. In some cases, smaller detachments suffice for a surprise, as illustrated by Prince Eugene's attempt at Cremona or the Austrian success at Cosel.

The primary rule when planning a surprise attack is to obtain accurate intelligence regarding the town's fortifications and interior layout. Such knowledge allows for a focused assault on specific weak points, increasing the chance of success. The surprise at Glogau stands as an exemplary model of such an operation; it is widely regarded as a masterstroke and provides a worthy example for anyone considering similar endeavors. In contrast, the surprise of Prague, although effective, succeeded largely due to the scale and variety of attacks, which overwhelmed the garrison by forcing them to defend an extensive perimeter.

Cosel and Cremona, however, were secured through betrayal: Cosel fell when an officer defected and informed the Austrians that a section of the ditch had not been completed, allowing them to enter and capture the position.

For smaller fortifications, surprise attacks can be directed at the gates. Mortar fire should be used to batter specific gates while detachments are positioned at others to prevent the garrison from escaping. If cannons are employed, they must be strategically positioned to avoid exposure to enemy musket fire; otherwise, the artillery risks being overrun and captured, jeopardizing the entire operation.

OF COMBATS AND BATTLES.

The Austrian camp is so densely surrounded by light troops that mounting a surprise attack would be exceptionally difficult. Such vigilance and defensive positioning create formidable barriers against surprise maneuvers. When two armies are in close proximity, a decisive encounter is almost inevitable, unless one side holds an elevated or fortified position that discourages direct engagement and guards against surprise—a scenario that is rare for entire armies but occasionally seen with smaller detachments.

For a successful surprise on an enemy encampment, several conditions must be met. First, the enemy must be overconfident, perhaps relying excessively on the strength of his own troops or assuming his position is too secure to be threatened. He may place undue trust in reports from his scouts or spies or feel assured by the extensive patrols and alertness of his light troops. All these factors create a foundation for complacency, opening the door to a surprise attack. Before forming any concrete plan, however, it is essential to understand the terrain, the enemy's precise location, and the general layout of their camp. Each road leading toward the camp must be thoroughly scouted, allowing us to assess the best approach points and develop a structured strategy tailored to the situation.

Select only the most experienced chasseurs, especially those familiar with the roads, to lead each column. This local knowledge will be indispensable in guiding the troops accurately and avoiding any errors that could expose our movements prematurely. Above all, the operation's success hinges on maintaining complete secrecy; secrecy, as always, is the essence of all surprise maneuvers. To prevent any deserter from betraying our plans, the light troops should lead the march. Beyond ensuring loyalty within the ranks, these light troops will also keep the enemy's patrols at a safe distance, reducing the risk that they will detect our advance too soon.

It is crucial that all subordinate generals receive clear, detailed instructions regarding possible scenarios and know precisely how to respond to unexpected developments. If the enemy's camp is positioned on an open plain, the advanced guard should consist of dragoons. Once these dragoons are joined by the hussars, they can charge into the camp at full speed, creating immediate chaos and cutting down anyone in their path.

The entire army should closely support this initial wave, with the infantry at the forefront. Their primary objective is to target and disrupt the wings of the enemy's cavalry, weakening their defensive cohesion. The advance guard should initiate the attack roughly thirty minutes before dawn, creating maximum confusion at the break of day, while the main body of the army should remain no more than eight hundred yards behind, ready to reinforce immediately.

During the entire approach, absolute silence must be observed. Soldiers should be strictly forbidden from speaking unnecessarily, and all smoking should be banned, as the smallest spark could betray our location in the darkness.

Once the assault begins and dawn breaks, the infantry, organized into four to six columns, should advance directly into the heart of the enemy's camp to support the efforts of the advance guard. No firing should take place before dawn, as the risks of friendly fire in the dark are too high. However, as soon as daylight allows, artillery should target areas where the advance guard has yet to penetrate, especially focusing on the wings of the enemy cavalry. The goal here is to force the enemy cavalry to abandon their horses, especially if they haven't had time to prepare properly, which will throw them into further disarray.

The pursuit should continue beyond the enemy's

camp, with the entire cavalry force released to chase the fleeing troops and take full advantage of their panic and confusion. If the enemy has discarded their weapons in their haste to escape, leave a detachment in charge of securing the camp while the rest of the army continues the pursuit, avoiding the temptation to halt for plunder. Pressing the attack to its fullest potential is crucial, as such opportunities to completely rout an enemy are rare. Taking advantage of this moment can allow us to dominate the campaign, dictating the terms of engagement for the foreseeable future.

I encountered a near-perfect opportunity of this kind shortly before the Battle of Mollwitz. We approached Marshal de Neipperg's army undetected, as his forces were scattered across three villages. With the benefit of hindsight, I realize I should have deployed two columns to surround the village of Mollwitz and initiated an assault there. At the same time, I could have sent dragoons to the other two villages, where the Austrian cavalry was stationed, to create confusion and prevent the cavalry from organizing. Following these dragoons, I would have deployed infantry to block the cavalry from mounting. I have little doubt that, with these tactics, we could have effectively annihilated their entire force.

I have already discussed the essential steps for securing our own camp and protecting it from enemy incursions. However, if despite all precautions the enemy manages to approach, the immediate response should be to organize the troops in battle formation on their assigned positions. The cavalry should hold firm, maintaining its position and firing by platoons until dawn. As daylight breaks, the generals should assess the situation, determining whether an advance is advisable based on the condition of the cavalry and the overall state of the field.

In these critical moments, each general must be prepared to act independently, making decisions without waiting for direct orders from the commander in chief. Personally, I am committed to avoiding night attacks due to the inherent confusion that darkness brings. Most soldiers need the oversight of their officers and the motivation provided by discipline to perform their duties effectively, and darkness can undermine both.

Charles XII of Sweden provides an instructive example of the perils of night attacks. In 1715, he launched a night assault on Prince of Anhalt immediately after landing on the island of Rügen. The King of Sweden had specific reasons for this tactic; daylight would have revealed the limited size of his force—only 4,000 men—against the 20,000 troops of his enemy. Despite the element of surprise, this numerical disadvantage ultimately led to his defeat, underscoring the risks of such endeavors.

An unchanging principle of warfare is to secure your flanks and rear while attempting to turn those of the enemy. This strategy can be executed in several ways, but they all share the same underlying goal: to outmaneuver the opponent and place them in a disadvantageous position.

When faced with the need to attack an entrenched enemy, the assault should be launched without delay to prevent the enemy from completing their fortifications. What may be an advantage today could turn against you by tomorrow if the enemy has time to strengthen their defenses.

However, before committing to the attack, it is essential to personally survey the enemy's position and determine its strengths and weaknesses. This close inspection will help you assess whether your initial plan is feasible or whether the task will require considerable effort and resources. A firsthand reconnaissance ensures that your approach is grounded in accurate knowledge of the terrain and enemy positioning.

Often, the main reason entrenchments are breached is due to inadequate support. Historical examples illustrate this well: the fortifications held by Turenne were captured due to insufficient support, as was another notable entrenchment because Prince of Anhalt could outflank it. Similarly, at the Battle of Malplaquet, the allied forces managed to breach Marshal Villars' left flank by utilizing a wooded area. If the allies had recognized this vulnerability sooner, they could have spared their army a loss of fifteen thousand soldiers.

If a river that can be forded provides support to an enemy entrenchment, then that side of the defense becomes the logical target for an attack. For instance, the Swedish fortifications at Stralsund were overcome because the attack was directed from the sea, where the defenses were vulnerable due to shallow waters.

When the enemy's fortifications are extensive, stretching their forces thin across a broad front, the best approach is to attack at multiple points. If our plans can be concealed from the enemy, preventing them from reinforcing any one area sufficiently, we increase our chances of penetrating their defenses. Such a strategy, when executed well, disrupts the enemy's defensive cohesion and enhances the likelihood of capturing key positions.

Consider the following hypothetical formation for an assault on an entrenched position. Picture a line formed by thirty battalions, with the left wing fortified by the river N. N. The primary assault will focus on the left, where we intend to break through with twelve battalions, while a supporting attack will be carried out on the right with eight battalions. The troops assigned to these attacks will form in a checkerboard pattern, ensuring adequate spacing between units for flexibility. The remaining infantry will form a third line, positioned at the center to reinforce as needed. Four hundred yards behind this line, the cavalry will be stationed, ready to exploit any weakness in the enemy's defense.

The presence of these infantry lines will serve to keep the enemy occupied and prevent them from reinforcing threatened areas. Additionally, the cavalry positioned in the rear will be prepared to seize upon any missteps made by the opposing forces, such as an overextension or shift in defense.

Each attacking force should be closely followed by a contingent of pioneers equipped with shovels, pickaxes, and fascines. Their task is to fill in ditches and clear paths, creating access points for the cavalry once the entrenchment is breached. These support units play a crucial role in ensuring the attack's success by enabling the cavalry to move through the enemy's fortifications smoothly.

The infantry designated for the assault should refrain from firing until they have overtaken the enemy's fortifications and are properly arrayed on the parapet in battle formation. Maintaining silence and restraint during the approach can provide the advantage of surprise and limit the enemy's awareness of our exact position and strength.

Once breaches are made in the entrenchments by the pioneers, the cavalry should enter through these gaps and engage the enemy with force. Timing is critical here—the cavalry must wait until a sufficient number of troops have penetrated the enemy lines and consolidated their position within the entrenchments. Then, with the pioneers' groundwork complete, the cavalry can deliver a decisive blow, exploiting the vulnerabilities created by the infantry's assault.

By executing each phase of this plan with precision and coordination, the assault on an entrenched enemy can disrupt even the most fortified positions, using the advantages of surprise, careful planning, and concerted force to overcome resistance.

If the cavalry is forced to retreat, they should regroup under cover from the infantry's fire, maintaining their position until the rest of the army has moved in, and the enemy has been fully routed. I must emphasize here that I would generally avoid entrenching my army unless a siege is underway or anticipated. Even then, I am inclined to believe it may be more advantageous to advance before the arrival of a relieving force rather than fortify too heavily.

However, if there is indeed a need to entrench, the following approach would be the most effective. In constructing a fortified position, we would establish two or three substantial reserve units positioned to deploy rapidly to any point where the enemy mounts a strong attack. These reserves serve as mobile support, reinforcing sections of the line under the greatest pressure.

The main parapet should be lined with battalions, with a reserve force stationed immediately behind them to provide support when needed. Positioned further back, the cavalry should be organized in a single line behind these reserves, ready to respond swiftly to any breach or weakness in the defense.

The entrenchments themselves must be thoroughly fortified. If there is a river along one side of the line, the ditch should extend into the river, preventing the enemy from easily outflanking the position. Where the fortifications border a wooded area, the defensive line should end in a redoubt, and a thick abatis (a barricade of felled trees) should be created within the forest to further reinforce that side.

Particular attention must be paid to the flanking capabilities of any redans (angled fortifications). The ditch should be dug as wide and as deep as possible, while the entrenchments should be improved daily. Reinforcements to the parapet, palisades at barrier entrances, deepened pits, and chevaux de frise (spiked barricades) around the entire camp all serve to strengthen the position incrementally.

The most significant advantage in defensive entrenchments lies in selecting the appropriate structure and adhering to sound fortification principles, which will force the enemy to attack from a narrow front and focus only on the key points of the defense line. For example, an illustration on Plate 7 shows an entrenched army positioned near a river. Here, the layout angles the front line outward toward the approaching enemy, creating a natural projection. Batteries positioned at the far end of the right flank prevent attacks from that direction, as these batteries would rake the enemy's flank, while a central redoubt would hit the attackers from the rear. Consequently, the center redoubt becomes the only feasible target for assault, but even here, the enemy must cut through a thick abatis before they can engage.

Given these defenses, the fortifications of the center redoubt should be reinforced heavily. By concentrating our attention and resources on one key point, we ensure that this critical part of the defense is as solid and secure as possible.

Alternatively, Plate 8 demonstrates a different fortification style, with alternating projecting and recessed redoubts linked by entrenchments. This configuration requires fewer but strategically positioned redoubts, making it possible to complete the defenses in less time while maintaining strength at the crucial points of potential attack.

In such projecting redoubts, the musketry fire should be planned so that it crosses, creating overlapping fields of fire that trap the enemy in a deadly cross-fire. To maintain this coverage, the redoubts should be spaced no more than six hundred yards apart.

Our infantry, defending the entrenchments, should rely on battalion volleys, with each soldier supplied with one hundred rounds. This ammunition supply is complemented by artillery, as many cannons as possible positioned between the battalions and within the projecting redoubts.

When the enemy is still at a distance, we use solid shot, firing to weaken them before they come within effective range. Once they close to within four hundred yards, we switch to grapeshot and canister, intensifying our defense as they near the entrenchment.

If, despite the strong defenses and steady, intense fire, the enemy manages to press forward and make a dent in our line, the infantry reserves must advance to push them back. Should this line of defense falter, the final counterattack rests with the cavalry, who charge forward as a last effort to drive the enemy into retreat.

Entrenchments typically fall for a few critical reasons: poor adherence to established fortification rules, a failure to effectively cover flanks, panic within the ranks, or the enemy's ability to outmaneuver the defenders. The attacking force often benefits from greater freedom of movement and confidence, which gives them a distinct advantage in overcoming fixed defensive positions.

Historical examples have demonstrated that once an entrenched position is breached, the entire defending army can quickly become demoralized and may even retreat in disarray. While I have complete faith in the resilience of my troops and their willingness to rally and repel the enemy, such determination would be wasted if the entrenchments themselves prevent us from exploiting any advantages gained. Entrenchments, while seemingly beneficial, can often impose limitations on an army's freedom of movement, making it challenging to capitalize on unexpected breakthroughs and limiting the possibility of strategic counterattacks.

Given these inherent disadvantages, it stands to reason that continuous defensive lines covering a large front are even more ineffective. These long lines of defense, although popular in recent military tactics, serve more to create vulnerabilities than to offer substantial protection. The style currently in vogue follows the approach of Prince Louis of Baden, who first implemented such defensive lines along the Briel. Later, the French employed a similar approach in Flanders, hoping that extensive lines would deter invasion. I maintain, however, that such defensive lines are more detrimental than beneficial. They require a broader span than the troops can realistically defend, creating gaps and weak spots where the enemy can easily break through. Instead of creating a secure front, these lines tempt the enemy into aggressive attacks and increase the likelihood of failure. Rather than protecting territory, they expose our forces to reputational damage should the line falter under pressure.

In warfare, numerical disadvantage need not lead to defeat, especially when sound tactics and intelligent maneuvering are employed. When facing a larger enemy force, a smaller army should aim to position itself in difficult, mountainous terrain where narrow passes and limited space neutralize the advantage of larger numbers. By restricting the enemy's ability to spread its forces and fully utilize its wings, we effectively level the playing field, making the numerical disparity less relevant. Such terrain provides natural choke points, creating opportunities to ambush the enemy, slow their movements, and limit the effectiveness of their formations. In close, hilly regions, we gain the added benefit of strengthened flanks, a distinct advantage compared to open plains where there is less natural cover. In fact, we secured victory at the Battle of Sohr largely due to our favorable positioning. Although the Austrian forces vastly outnumbered ours, they were unable to break through our flanks, as the terrain kept their superior numbers from becoming an insurmountable threat.

Choosing the most advantageous ground is my first priority, as the right terrain can fundamentally shift the odds in battle. Following the selection of ground, my focus turns to arranging the battle disposition itself. Here, my preferred tactic is the oblique order of battle, an approach that offers a means of both defensive and offensive maneuvering. In this arrangement, we refuse one wing to the enemy, keeping it out of the main engagement, while reinforcing the other wing, which is tasked with leading the attack. Concentrating our forces on a single point enables us to turn the enemy's flank and launch a decisive blow where they are weakest.

An army of even ten thousand men, if its flanks are turned effectively, will find itself rapidly encircled and at risk of collapse. The maneuver centers on the actions of the right wing, where all our offensive power is directed. First, a body of infantry is sent forward to infiltrate the wooded area on the flank, striking at the enemy cavalry from the side and creating a gap for our own cavalry to exploit. Meanwhile, a regiment of hussars charges into the enemy's rear, further destabilizing their line and causing confusion. As the enemy cavalry is broken and begins to retreat, our infantry advances from the woods, flanking the enemy's infantry, while the rest of our forces press the attack head-on.

Meanwhile, the left wing remains stationary, preserving its strength until the enemy's left wing is fully routed. This coordinated approach achieves multiple strategic objectives. Firstly, it enables a smaller force to hold its own against a much larger opponent, as the focus is on exploiting weaknesses rather than matching strength with strength. Secondly, it allows us to concentrate our attack on a single, decisive point that, once breached, has the potential to unravel the enemy's entire formation. Thirdly, if our attacking wing is repulsed, the remainder of our forces remains intact, with three-fourths of our troops still fresh and available to cover a strategic withdrawal, should it become necessary.

When confronting an enemy holding a naturally advantageous position, it is critical to carefully assess both strong and weak points before making any move. The goal should always be to identify the area of least resistance and direct the attack there, maximizing efficiency and minimizing unnecessary losses. Attacks on fortified villages, for example, are often unreasonably costly. Such actions typically result in high casualties among our best infantry, which weakens the overall force. For this reason, I avoid attacking villages unless it is absolutely unavoidable. Villages often serve as a trap, consuming resources and soldiers in a battle for limited gains while risking significant losses.

Some military theorists suggest that the center of the enemy's position is the most effective target, arguing that a successful penetration there will cause the enemy's entire formation to buckle. For instance, if an enemy position includes two large towns and two villages on its wings, then capturing the center will cause a ripple effect, leading to the inevitable fall of the flanks. Plate 10 illustrates such a situation, where a break in the center exposes the wings, leading to their eventual collapse. This approach, when properly executed, has the potential to yield a complete and sweeping victory by exploiting the inherent weakness in the enemy's structure.

Once a breach is made in the center, the attack should be intensified, pressuring the enemy to retreat from both the right and left sides. There is no greater asset in such an assault than the concentrated fire of artillery loaded with cartridges, which devastates the enemy's battalions. The powerful effect of artillery fire was evident during the battles at Sohr and Kesselsdorf, where attacks on well-defended batteries taught me valuable lessons in the complexities of capturing fortified gun positions. For example, let us imagine attempting to capture a heavily fortified battery with fifteen cannons that cannot be outflanked. In such situations, a frontal assault would likely result in devastating losses, as the combined fire of artillery and infantry makes it nearly impregnable. Capturing such a position often depends more on enemy error than on brute force.

In these cases, as our infantry mounts an attack, they are often repulsed, prompting the enemy's defenders to abandon their posts temporarily in pursuit. This movement leaves the artillery momentarily undefended, creating an opportunity for our forces to regroup and push forward. The defenders, realizing their mistake, then attempt to return to their guns, only to find our troops seizing control alongside them.

To improve our chances in such scenarios, I devised a specific maneuver based on experiences from these engagements. The attacking forces are arranged in two lines with a checkerboard formation, supported by a third line of dragoons. The first line advances with a light attack, designed to draw a response without engaging fully. Once contact is made, this line falls back through gaps in the second line, feigning retreat and enticing the defenders to abandon their position to pursue. At this point, we launch a vigorous, coordinated assault, using the defenders' momentary lapse to overrun the position.

This tactic aligns with a guiding principle: never place undue reliance on any single position unless it is unequivocally secure against all foreseeable threats. The primary strength of our troops lies in their offensive capability. Ceding this advantage without sufficient cause would undermine our fundamental tactical approach.

When occupying defensive positions becomes necessary, the priority should be to secure high ground, as elevation offers inherent strategic value. Additionally, reinforcing the flanks is essential to prevent the enemy from finding weak spots. If there are villages situated at the head or on the flanks of our position, it would be prudent to burn them, provided the wind direction does not drive smoke into our own camp. Destroying these villages prevents the enemy from using them as cover and disrupts any planned approach, further strengthening our position and enhancing the defense's overall effectiveness. By adhering to these principles and maintaining flexibility in both offensive and defensive operations, we can maximize our chances of success in any engagement, regardless of the size or positioning of opposing forces.

If there are any solid stone buildings situated in front of the main line, I would station infantry within them to harass and impede the enemy during the engagement. Such structures offer natural defensive benefits and can serve as strong points to delay or disrupt the enemy's advance.

It is critical, however, to avoid placing troops on terrain where they cannot effectively operate. Our position at Grotkau in 1741 was rendered nearly useless because the center and left wing were posted behind impassable bogs. The only usable ground, where any maneuvering could take place, was occupied by a portion of the right wing. This misalignment cost us strategically, limiting the effectiveness of our formation. Similarly, Villeroy's defeat at the Battle of Ramillies occurred because his right wing was positioned in such a way that it became ineffective, leaving the entire French force vulnerable when the enemy concentrated their attack against the unsupported right flank.

While I encourage Prussian troops to occupy advantageous positions as other armies do, these positions should serve a temporary purpose. Once these positions have been used to favor a movement or secure artillery support, the troops must vacate them promptly to engage the enemy directly. Rather than allowing the enemy to initiate an attack, we turn the tables, attacking them instead and thwarting their plans. Any unexpected movement we make in the enemy's presence is almost certain to yield positive results, particularly when directed against a weak or exposed point.

I consider battles fought in this manner to be among the most effective engagements. On these occasions, I would order the infantry to refrain from firing as it only slows their advance. Victory in these encounters is not measured by the number of casualties inflicted but by the extent of ground gained. The surest path to victory is to march forward swiftly and in tight formation, continuously advancing and pressing the enemy. When moving through challenging, broken terrain, it is customary to allow an interval of fifteen yards between squadrons. However, on even ground, the line should be unbroken, forming a solid front.

For the infantry, the spacing should be just wide enough to allow room for the artillery. Exceptions are made only in certain scenarios—such as assaults on entrenchments, batteries, or villages, and in forming the rear guard during a retreat—where cavalry and infantry are arranged in a checkerboard formation. This pattern allows the second line to immediately fill any gaps in the first, providing support and enabling an orderly retreat, with each unit able to cover the other as they withdraw. This principle is fundamental and should never be overlooked.

This discussion provides an opportunity to outline some core principles for arranging an army in battle formation, regardless of the terrain. First, select prominent landmarks as reference points for aligning the wings. For instance, the right wing might align itself with a particular steeple designated as point N.N. The commanding general must exercise extreme caution in ensuring that the troops do not establish their positions incorrectly, as even a slight misalignment can disrupt the entire formation.

It is not always necessary to delay the attack until the full army is ready to engage. At times, opportunities arise that can be exploited swiftly, and hesitation could result in losing a strategic advantage. While a large portion of the army should generally be engaged in the battle, the first line should receive primary consideration when establishing the order of battle. If any regiments in the first line are unavailable, they should be replaced with an equal number from the second line to maintain continuity.

Special attention should be given to the wings, especially those expected to bear the brunt of the engagement. In open terrain, where the enemy is free to maneuver, it is essential to maintain a uniformly strong order of battle throughout the line. The enemy may hold back a reserve force, which they could deploy to disrupt our formation, so all parts of the line must be equally prepared to respond to potential threats.

If one wing lacks adequate support, the general commanding the second line should immediately dispatch dragoons to extend and reinforce the first line, without waiting for formal orders. Meanwhile, hussars from the third line can take the place of the dragoons, ensuring that the reinforcement does not weaken the second line's overall integrity.

This maneuver is critical because, should the enemy attempt to flank the first line's cavalry, the dragoons and hussars will be in position to counter the enemy's move and return the threat, ensuring that our forces remain adaptable and resilient in the face of unexpected developments.

To support the left wing, I recommend positioning three battalions in the interval between the two lines, as this will provide additional security. In the event that our cavalry is repulsed, these battalions will serve as a barrier, preventing the enemy from advancing directly onto the infantry—a tactic that proved effective during the Battle of Mollwitz.

The general in command of the second line should maintain a distance of three hundred paces from the first line. If he notices any gaps or intervals forming in the first line, he should promptly deploy battalions from the second line to fill them. This proactive approach ensures continuity in the battle formation, preventing weaknesses that the enemy could exploit.

In an open plain, it's advantageous to station a reserve cavalry unit behind the center of the infantry battalions. This reserve should be led by a capable officer who can operate independently, either reinforcing a pressured wing or flanking the enemy in pursuit if they manage to disorder one of our wings. This reserve gives the cavalry a moment to rally and reorganize while protecting the main force.

To initiate the engagement, the cavalry should charge at full gallop, while the infantry advances briskly toward the enemy. Commanding officers must ensure their troops penetrate and break through the enemy lines entirely. It is crucial that no one fires until the enemy is clearly routed, as premature firing can disrupt the momentum of the attack. Should any soldiers fire without orders, they must be immediately commanded to shoulder arms and resume their march without pausing. Once the enemy begins to falter, we can allow firing by battalions, which, when coordinated, can bring the engagement to a swift conclusion.

This formation includes a unique feature where small bodies of infantry are positioned at the extremities of the cavalry wings. These battalions provide support by using their own cannons, along with those on the cavalry wings, to target the enemy's cavalry from the outset, giving our cavalry an advantage as they prepare to charge. Additionally, if our wings are forced to retreat, the enemy's pursuit will be deterred by the risk of being caught between two fires—our main line and these supporting battalions.

When our cavalry appears to have gained the upper hand, this supporting infantry should advance toward the enemy's infantry. The battalions positioned in the intervals between the cavalry units should then quarter-wheel, moving to the flanks and rear of the enemy infantry, allowing us to surround and decisively engage them.

The victorious cavalry wing must prevent the enemy's cavalry from regrouping, pursuing them in orderly fashion and cutting them off from their own infantry. As confusion overtakes the enemy, the commanding officer should dispatch hussars to pursue the routed troops, supported by our main cavalry force. At the same time, dragoons should be sent along the roads the enemy infantry is using to retreat, capturing as many as possible and disrupting any organized escape.

This order of battle introduces another element—integrating dragoon squadrons with the infantry of the second line. In past engagements with Austrian forces, I observed that after approximately fifteen minutes of musket fire, Austrian soldiers tend to gather around their colors in small, dense formations. During the Battle of Hohenfriedburg, our cavalry exploited this tendency by charging these clusters, capturing many prisoners in the process. With the dragoons positioned nearby, they can immediately charge into these groups when the opportunity arises, leading to effective captures and disrupting enemy cohesion.

Some may argue that I appear to rely heavily on artillery over small arms in these dispositions. My response is that one of two outcomes is nearly inevitable: either our infantry will fire despite orders not to, or they will hold fire, waiting for the enemy to waver. In either case, the moment confusion is observed among the enemy, the cavalry should be ordered to charge. Facing flanking attacks on one side, a frontal assault on the other, and a cut-off line of retreat, most enemy troops will inevitably surrender or be captured.

In such a situation, the battle becomes less a contest and more a complete rout, especially if no natural obstacle, such as a defile, exists to shield the enemy's retreat.

In marching to battle, whether advancing by the right or left, the battalions or divisions must remain closely aligned, ensuring they are ready to engage as soon as they deploy. If advancing in a broad front, careful attention must be paid to maintain appropriate spacing, so that units are neither too tightly clustered nor too far apart.

There is also a distinction between positioning heavy artillery and field pieces attached to battalions. Heavy cannons should be stationed on elevated terrain, while the battalion field pieces should be set fifty paces ahead of the infantry. All artillery, regardless of type, must be well-aimed and consistently fired to maximize impact.

As the line advances to within five hundred yards of the enemy, field artillery should be moved by hand, allowing for uninterrupted firing. Once the enemy is in full retreat, the heavy artillery should also advance, firing a few more rounds as a parting blow to ensure their departure remains chaotic.

Each piece of artillery in the first line should be manned by six gunners, along with three regimental carpenters to maintain and operate the equipment efficiently. At approximately three hundred and fifty yards, artillery should switch to firing cartridges for maximum effect as the enemy is within critical range.

Victory in battle requires more than defeating the enemy in the immediate sense; it demands understanding how to capitalize on that victory fully. To spill blood needlessly, without securing a strategic advantage, is wasteful and inhumane. Pursuing a retreating enemy to heighten their fear and capture prisoners not only determines the current engagement but influences the course of future encounters. However, practical limitations— such as a shortage of provisions or troop exhaustion—may sometimes prevent a full pursuit. These factors must always be weighed carefully to balance immediate gains against the needs of sustaining the campaign over time.

It is ultimately the responsibility of the commanding general if an army finds itself lacking in provisions. When he chooses to engage in battle, he does so with a specific purpose in mind; and having such a purpose obliges him to ensure that all necessary preparations are in place to achieve it. This includes having a sufficient supply of bread or biscuits to sustain the army for eight to ten days. Such planning is essential to maintaining momentum and avoiding logistical setbacks that could undermine the success of the campaign.

As for the physical demands on the soldiers, any hardships they endure should not be given undue consideration if those exertions contribute to the attainment of victory. In times of exceptional opportunity, it is expected that the troops will be called upon to perform extraordinary feats, accepting the rigors of such efforts as part of their duty.

Once victory has been decisively secured, I recommend dispatching a detachment from among the regiments that have suffered the greatest losses. This group's mission would be to care for the wounded, prioritizing our own but extending basic care to enemy casualties as well. These soldiers should be transported to the hospitals, which, ideally, have already been set up in advance, demonstrating foresight in caring for the casualties.

Meanwhile, the main army should not hesitate to press on and pursue the defeated enemy to the nearest defile. In their state of panic, they are unlikely to maintain control of such positions if they are immediately pursued. The pursuit must be relentless to prevent the enemy from catching their breath and regrouping; otherwise, they might turn these natural defenses to their advantage.

After securing this initial victory and attending to the aftermath, it is time to establish the camp. When doing so, strict adherence to established rules and security measures is essential; overconfidence can be a grave miscalculation. Even when the victory appears complete, we should not assume that the enemy has no fight left. They may still have the resources or cunning to seize upon any negligence or error in our ranks, and vigilance is crucial to prevent this.

In cases of an absolute victory, additional steps can be taken to maximize the gains. Detachments may be dispatched to intercept the enemy's retreat routes, seize their supply depots, or even lay siege to multiple towns simultaneously. Here, specific strategies depend largely on the situation at hand, as circumstances beyond control often influence the best course of action. One must remember that as long as there is more to accomplish, the task is not finished. A sharp-minded, defeated enemy will seize any opportunity to exploit lapses in our conduct.

I earnestly hope the Prussian forces will never know defeat and am confident that, with sound leadership and rigorous discipline, they will avoid such a fate.

However, should such a misfortune befall them, there are specific actions that can help mitigate its impact and restore the army's footing.

When it becomes evident that a battle is lost and that the enemy's advances are unavoidable, immediate steps should be taken to secure a controlled retreat. First, the second line of infantry should be sent to any nearby defile to establish a defensive position, utilizing the principles outlined in the section on retreats. Along with the infantry, as many cannons as can be spared should be stationed at this point to strengthen the line.

If no such natural chokepoint is available, the first line should retreat through the intervals in the second line, reforming into battle formation approximately three hundred yards behind. This spacing allows for an orderly fallback, providing a buffer for regrouping. The remaining cavalry must be consolidated and, if desired, can be arranged into a square formation. Such a formation offers greater defensive resilience, shielding the retreating forces from enemy incursions.

History offers notable examples of this tactic. After the Battle of Frauenstadt, General Schullembourg used a square formation to lead his forces across the Oder River without interference from Charles XII. Similarly, after the first Battle of Hochstädt, the Prince of Anhalt deployed his forces in a square to withdraw across a two-league plain, deterring the French cavalry from engaging them. These cases illustrate how, even in defeat, maintaining composure and using strategic formations can protect an army's integrity during retreat.

Finally, I emphasize that a defeat does not necessitate a long and frantic retreat of forty leagues or more. Rather, the army should withdraw only to the nearest advantageous position, rallying there to regain cohesion and morale. By taking up a defensible position and projecting confidence, the army can gather its scattered ranks and provide reassurance to those who are disheartened. This immediate regrouping prevents an initial setback from devolving into a complete rout and keeps the army poised for future engagements.

OF THE REASONS WHICH SHOULD INDUCE US TO GIVE BATTLE, AND IN WHAT MANNER IT IS TO BE CONDUCTED.

Battles shape the fate of nations. It is essential that they be decisive, whether the goal is to free ourselves from the ongoing burdens of war, place the enemy in a disadvantaged state, or resolve a conflict that might otherwise persist indefinitely. A wise commander will not make any movement without a sound reason, and a general should never engage his forces in battle unless he has a strategic objective of considerable importance. If he finds himself forced into battle by his opponent, it is likely due to previous errors that have allowed the enemy to dictate the terms and place him at a disadvantage.

Reflecting on my own experience, I do not claim infallibility. Out of five battles fought by my troops, only three were intentionally planned, while in two instances, circumstances forced me into conflict. At Mollwitz, for instance, the Austrians had positioned themselves between my army and Wohlau, where I kept my provisions and artillery, necessitating a battle to maintain access to essential resources. Similarly, at Sohr, the enemy had cut off my route to Trautenau, leaving me no choice but to fight or risk the loss of my entire force. The contrast between battles we choose and those imposed upon us is striking. The premeditated battles of Hohen-Friedberg, Kesselsdorf, and Czaslau yielded brilliant victories, with the engagement at Czaslau even leading to a negotiated peace.

In setting forth these guidelines for battle, I do not deny that I have made my own share of errors through oversight. However, I expect my officers to learn from these mistakes, and they can be assured that I am committed to rectifying them through diligent study and improved tactics.

There are instances when both armies may desire engagement, leading to a swift and decisive resolution. However, the most advantageous battles are those in which we compel the enemy to fight against his will. It is a fundamental principle of warfare to force the enemy into actions he would rather avoid. Since our interests and the enemy's are naturally opposed, it is unlikely that both of us desire the same outcome from a confrontation.

Numerous factors might compel us to engage in battle: the need to force the enemy to lift a siege on a strategically valuable location, to drive him from a province he occupies, to penetrate further into his territory, to gain the upper hand in a siege, to press him toward peace negotiations, or to capitalize on any mistake he has made. For example, if we maneuver to threaten a town of importance to him or sever his lines of communication, the enemy may be forced into a confrontation to protect his interests.

In conducting such maneuvers, however, we must be cautious not to place ourselves in a similar predicament, as overextending our forces or occupying a position vulnerable to counterattacks could give the enemy the same opportunities against us. Engagements targeting an enemy's rear guard often carry the least risk, as they can disrupt his movements without exposing our own forces to undue danger.

If such a strategy is pursued, the most effective approach is to encamp near the enemy and wait for an opportunity when he attempts to withdraw through defiles or narrow passages. At that moment, we can strike his rear guard, potentially securing a decisive advantage with minimal risk. Small-scale engagements like these can yield substantial gains and often produce outcomes disproportionate to their scope.

There is also the tactic of harassing the enemy to disrupt his ability to consolidate scattered forces. The purpose of this strategy is justified by the objective at hand, although a skilled enemy may counter it with a rapid forced march or by positioning himself in an advantageous spot to avoid interception. On occasion, we may also find ourselves drawn into battle by the enemy's missteps. When the opposing force makes an error, it is our duty to capitalize on it, as every fault in the enemy's plan presents an opportunity to punish his lack of prudence.

Moreover, it is essential to keep in mind that our wars should be as brief and decisive as possible. Prolonged engagements are not in our interest, as they gradually weaken discipline, deplete the population, and exhaust the nation's resources. Consequently, Prussian generals should strive to conclude campaigns with a balance of prudence and urgency. Success should not tempt us to delay; instead, we must act efficiently to secure a quick and strategic conclusion.

The Marshal de Luxembourg's response during the Flanders campaigns is a cautionary tale. When his son suggested that they could capture yet another town, Luxembourg replied dismissively, "Hold your tongue, you little fool! Would you have us go home to plant cabbages?" Such complacency risks prolonging conflict without purpose. Rather, we should adopt the philosophy of the Hebrew leader Sennacherib, who believed it better to sacrifice one man than to risk the well-being of an entire people.

There are instances in military history that illustrate the principle of exploiting an enemy's mistake. In the Battle of Senef, the Prince of Condé seized the opportunity to engage the rear guard of the Prince of Orange (or possibly Prince of Waldeck) when he failed to secure the entrance to a defile, making his retreat vulnerable. The battle accounts of Marshal de Luxembourg's unnamed victory, as well as the Battle of Raucoux, provide further examples of how adept generals have capitalized on enemy errors.

In sum, battles are complex affairs with far-reaching consequences, and every engagement must be approached with purpose, preparation, and a readiness to exploit any advantage. By understanding and applying these principles, we can increase our chances of achieving not only victory in battle but also a swift and favorable resolution to the larger conflict.

ARTICLE XXII

OF THE HAZARDS AND UNFORESEEN ACCIDENTS WHICH HAPPEN IN WAR

This discussion would become unmanageably lengthy if we delved into every possible mishap a general might encounter in war. To summarize, a general needs both skill and good fortune to succeed. Generals face far more challenges and scrutiny than most people realize. Their actions are judged by the public, often based on nothing more than a brief report in the gazette, while the very readers passing judgment may lack even the basic experience to lead a small detachment, let alone command an army.

I don't aim to excuse generals who have made errors—my own campaign in 1744, for instance, had its share of missteps. But while I've often made mistakes, I have also undertaken successful operations, such as the siege of Prague, the defense and retreat at Koelin, and another strategic retreat in Silesia. I won't detail these campaigns further here, but it's important to acknowledge that some misfortunes cannot be avoided, no matter how well- planned or carefully considered the strategy may be.

Since these notes are intended for my generals, I'll

focus on lessons from my own experiences rather than other examples. At Reichenbach, I planned a forced march to reach the Neiss River, intending to cut off General de Neuperg's communication by positioning my forces between his army and the town of Neiss. All preparations were in place, but heavy rain turned the roads to mud, stalling our advance guard and preventing the pontoons from moving forward. A dense fog compounded the issue, leaving village guards lost and unable to rejoin their regiments. The conditions were so poor that, rather than arriving at 4 a.m. as planned, we reached the river at midnight. By that time, the element of surprise was lost; the enemy had already prepared for our approach, and the opportunity slipped away.

Disease can also derail the best-laid plans. During our campaign in Bohemia in 1741, poor provisions led to sickness among the troops, forcing us into a defensive position. In another instance, at Hohen-Friedberg, I dispatched an aide-de-camp to instruct Margrave Charles to command the second line, as General Kalckstein had been detached to lead the right wing against the Saxons. Unfortunately, the aide misunderstood and instructed the Margrave to reorganize the first line into the second, a miscommunication that could have thrown our lines into complete disarray had I not discovered it in time to correct the error.

These examples underscore the importance of staying vigilant and recognizing that a single poorly executed order can disrupt an entire strategy. If a general commanding a critical detachment falls ill or is killed, it can create substantial complications for the overarching battle plan. Offensive maneuvers, in particular, demand generals of both sound judgment and unwavering courage, qualities that are rare; in my entire army, I count no more than three or four such individuals.

Even with the best precautions, losing a critical convoy to the enemy can ruin a plan, requiring either a significant pause or a complete reevaluation. Should circumstances necessitate a retreat, the troops may become demoralized. While I have fortunately not experienced such a setback with my entire army, I observed this effect at the Battle of Mollwitz. After a setback, it took considerable effort to revive the spirits of the troops, especially the cavalry, which was so shaken that they seemed resigned to defeat. To restore their morale, I sent out small detachments to give them a manageable task and gradually ease them back into combat readiness. It was not until the Battle of Hohen-Friedberg that our cavalry regained the confidence and effectiveness they continue to exhibit today.

The discovery of a significant spy within the enemy's camp can deal a severe blow to one's intelligence efforts. Without such informants, a general must rely solely on personal observation, a limitation that restricts insight into the enemy's movements and intentions.

The carelessness of officers tasked with reconnaissance can also create distressing complications. Marshal de Neuperg, for example, was taken by surprise when a hussar officer, assigned to keep watch, neglected his duties, allowing our forces to approach undetected. Similarly, an officer from the regiment of Ziethen failed to conduct his night patrol properly, enabling the enemy to build bridges at Selmitz and surprise our baggage train.

War is fraught with unpredictable challenges, and while one must be prepared for setbacks, many factors remain beyond a general's control. That said, by anticipating potential issues, staying alert to changing conditions, and instilling responsibility in subordinates, we can better navigate the many hazards of command. Through these reflections, I hope to equip my officers with the resilience and adaptability necessary to mitigate the effects of unforeseen setbacks, maintaining both the integrity of the army and the momentum of the campaign.

This illustrates the importance of my belief that the security of an entire army should never rest solely on the vigilance of a single officer. Entrusting such a consequential responsibility to one man, particularly a lower-ranking officer, is an unwarranted risk. Remember carefully the guidance I have given on this matter under the topic "Of the Defence of Rivers." It is essential to rely not solely on patrols and reconnaissance parties, but on strategies that provide stronger, more reliable safeguards.

Of all the disasters that can befall an army, treason is the most perilous. A notorious example occurred in 1733 when Prince Eugene was betrayed by General St. . . ., who had been bribed by the French. I, too, have felt the sting of betrayal; the fortress of Cosel was lost due to the treachery of a garrison officer who defected and led the enemy directly to it. Such examples serve as a stern reminder that, even when fortune seems firmly on our side, we should be wary of complacency and refrain from letting success breed overconfidence. Instead, we should remain mindful that any skill or foresight we claim is, at best, subject to the whims of unforeseen events—forces beyond our control that seem determined, for reasons unknown, to humble even the proudest of human plans.

ARTICLE XXIII

IF IT BE ABSOLUTELY NECESSARY THAT THE GENERAL OF AN ARMY SHOULD HOLD A COUNCIL OF WAR.

Prince Eugene once remarked that "if a general does not wish to fight, he only needs to hold a council of war." His point is well-proven, as councils of war tend almost universally to vote against engaging. In these settings, secrecy—so essential to military operations—is often lost, as too many opinions and details are shared openly.

A general, entrusted by his sovereign with command of the army, should act independently and decisively. The confidence placed in him by his king justifies such an approach. Yet, while a general must lead firmly, he should not disregard the counsel of even the lowest-ranking officer. In matters concerning the nation's welfare, a true patriot sets aside personal pride and considers all suggestions, valuing advice that may lead to the successful outcome they all strive for.

ARTICLE XXIV

OF THE MANOEUVRES OF AN ARMY.

The principles outlined in this work shed light on the theory behind the maneuvers I have instilled within my troops. These tactics are designed with the primary goal of maximizing every possible moment, enabling us to resolve engagements more swiftly than has been customary, and ultimately to overwhelm the enemy through the relentless momentum of our cavalry's charge. This intense, impetuous force ensures that even the most reluctant soldier is swept along, compelled to perform his duty alongside the bravest, making every trooper an active participant in the assault. Success relies heavily on the vigor of the attack.

With this in mind, I am confident that each general, fully appreciating the necessity and benefits of strict discipline, will prioritize its preservation and enhancement, both during wartime and in periods of peace. I am often reminded of the inspiring words of Vegetius regarding the Romans: "And finally," he declared, "Roman discipline triumphed over the hordes of Germans, the strength of the Gauls, the cunning of the Germans, the vast barbarian hosts, and conquered the entire world." Such is the importance of disciplined forces to the flourishing and security of a state.

ARTICLE XXV

OF WINTER QUARTERS.

When a campaign concludes, the focus naturally shifts to organizing winter quarters. This requires careful planning and must align with the unique circumstances at hand. The first priority in establishing winter quarters is to construct a robust protective chain around these positions. Such a defensive line can be created in several ways, depending on the available natural and constructed defenses: positioning the line behind a river, leveraging mountainous terrain for added security, or taking advantage of nearby fortified towns to serve as protective barriers.

During the winter of 1741-42, for example, when my forces wintered in Bohemia, we set up behind the Elbe River, with our protective chain beginning at Brandeis and extending through key points, including Nienbourg, Koelin, Pojebrod, and Pardubitz, eventually ending at Konigingraetz. However, it is important to remember that rivers are not impenetrable barriers. When frozen, they can be crossed at numerous points, which highlights the need for constant vigilance. For this reason, hussars should be stationed along the full length of the chain to observe the enemy's movements carefully. These hussars are responsible for patrolling frequently, monitoring for any unusual activity or signs of enemy troop gatherings in the area.

Beyond the infantry chain, additional brigades of both cavalry and infantry should be stationed at strategic intervals. This arrangement ensures a rapid response and provides reinforcement to any section that might require immediate assistance. In the winter of 1744-45, we secured our quarters by establishing a defensive line along the mountain range separating Silesia from Bohemia. We guarded this line meticulously, aiming to maintain peace within our quarters. Lieutenant-General de Trusches, for instance, oversaw the front of Lusatia up to the Glatz region, covering crucial posts from Sagan to Schmiedberg, extending to Friedland, where redoubts were fortified for additional defense. Additional fortified posts were constructed along the vital routes of Schatzlar, Liebau, and Silberberg, bolstered by a reserve unit, ready to assist any post that might come under attack.

To add further strength, abbatis were set up in the surrounding forests, creating blockages on all routes leading into Bohemia and thereby limiting enemy movement. Every post was also equipped with hussars, assigned specifically for reconnaissance duties, ensuring that any attempt by the enemy to advance would be immediately detected. General Lehwald similarly protected the Glatz region with his own defensive arrangements, fortified positions, and prudent precautions. He and General Trusches coordinated their efforts to provide mutual support. Thus, if the Austrians moved against General Trusches, General Lehwald could counter by advancing into Bohemia from the rear, and General Trusches would do the same if Lehwald's forces were threatened. This network of mutual defense ensured that neither general's position could be easily overwhelmed.

Tropau and Jagerndorf were significant posts in Upper Silesia, and the main line of communication with Glatz ran through Zeigenhals and Patchskau, while another route through Neustadt connected to Neiss. It is also prudent to avoid excessive reliance on mountainous terrain for security, as we must remember the adage, "Where a goat can pass, a soldier can follow." For those winter quarters that benefit from proximity to fortresses, Marshal Saxe's arrangements provide an excellent model. Yet, we cannot always choose the ideal positions, as our defensive lines must adapt to the geographical realities of the terrain we occupy.

It should be regarded as a fundamental principle that we are never to consider any location entirely safe from enemy incursions. A constant state of readiness is required to maintain security within our winter quarters. Another important practice is to assign regiments by brigades, keeping them under the direct supervision of their respective generals. Where possible, generals should remain close to their own regiments, providing oversight and ensuring that discipline and readiness are maintained. However, exceptions to this rule may be necessary at times, depending on the broader strategy and the army's needs, which the commanding general is best positioned to assess.

There are also logistical considerations to be addressed regarding the upkeep of troops during winter quarters. If circumstances demand that we take winter quarters within our own territory, captains and subordinate officers should be compensated to match what they would typically receive in occupied winter quarters.

Additionally, the soldiers should be provided with bread and meat at no cost to them, ensuring that their needs are met without imposing undue strain on their resources.

If, however, our winter quarters are in enemy territory, resource allocation follows a distinct structure. In this scenario, the commanding general receives an allowance of 15,000 florins, while generals of cavalry and infantry receive 10,000 florins each. Lieutenant-generals are allocated 7,000 florins, major-generals or camp marshals receive 5,000, cavalry captains are given 2,000, infantry captains 1,800, and subaltern officers between 1,000 ducats and 400-500 florins. Soldiers are provided with bread, meat, and beer without charge, though they are not issued money directly, as this could increase the risk of desertion.

The commanding general must closely monitor this allocation to prevent looting and to maintain order. Some leniency may be afforded to officers if they can secure small, fair gains, but plundering should be strictly controlled to maintain discipline and prevent resentment among the local populace. When stationed in enemy territory, the general must also ensure that an adequate number of recruits are obtained. The distribution process should be organized so that each district, or "circle," supplies a certain number of regiments. Ideally, each circle should be subdivided to match our cantonment arrangements, thereby streamlining the recruitment and training process.

If local authorities willingly supply recruits, that arrangement is preferable. If not, firmer methods may be required to meet recruitment needs. The early arrival of recruits is crucial, as it allows sufficient time for them to undergo training and become combat-ready by the spring. Captains should still send out additional recruiting parties if necessary to meet the numbers required.

The general must oversee all logistical aspects, such as securing artillery horses and other necessary supplies, either directly from the region or through compensation. Equipment maintenance is vital, and all military gear, from baggage wagons to basic supplies, should be repaired or replaced at the enemy's expense. This includes specific attention to the needs of the cavalry, whose officers must ensure saddles, bridles, stirrups, and boots are maintained in peak condition. Infantry officers, meanwhile, should ensure their men are supplied with adequate shoes, stockings, shirts, and gaiters for the next campaign. Soldiers' blankets and tents must be repaired, and cavalry swords sharpened, while infantry arms should be inspected and readied.

Additionally, artillery teams must prepare ample ammunition, especially cartridges for the infantry, to ensure our forces are fully equipped for the spring campaign. By attending meticulously to these logistical details, we can enter the next season with a well-prepared, well-provisioned, and confident army, ready for whatever engagements may come.

It remains essential for the general to ensure that all troops assigned to form the defensive chain are adequately supplied with powder and shot, and, indeed, that no essential provision is lacking for the entire army. Should time permit, it is highly advantageous for the general to visit various quarters himself. By doing so, he can assess the condition of the troops firsthand, ensuring that officers are diligently overseeing both the training and welfare of their men. Such oversight is vital, as regular drilling is necessary not only for recruits but also for seasoned soldiers to keep them sharp and ready for the demands of combat.

At the start of each campaign, the arrangement of cantonments is adjusted to align with the expected order of battle. Typically, this involves positioning the cavalry on the wings and placing the infantry at the center. These cantonments often extend nine to ten leagues (or about four to five miles) forward, with a depth of approximately four leagues (or two miles). As the time for encampment approaches, it becomes necessary to draw these cantonments inward slightly, consolidating the positions in preparation for rapid deployment.

A well-organized structure within the cantonments can significantly enhance the efficiency of command. I have found it highly practical to assign command responsibilities to the six senior-most generals. For instance, one general should oversee the cavalry on the right wing of the first line, while another commands the left. Similarly, two additional generals can command the cavalry of the second line, each responsible for a wing. This approach facilitates swift communication and execution of orders and enables the troops to asscmble into columns for camp or combat with greater ease and precision.

Concerning the subject of winter quarters, I must once again advise great caution in entering them prematurely. It is imperative to confirm beyond doubt that the enemy's forces have fully disbanded before settling into winter positions. Let the misfortune of Elector Frederick William serve as a reminder: he was caught off guard and surprised in his quarters in Alsace by Marshal de

Turenne, suffering a setback that might have been avoided with greater vigilance.

In sum, these strategies are not mere formalities but are fundamental to preserving the army's readiness, security, and overall effectiveness, ensuring that our forces are always prepared for rapid mobilization or engagement should the need arise.

ARTICLE XXVI

OF WINTER CAMPAIGNS IN PARTICULAR.

Winter campaigns are particularly taxing on troops, not only due to the illnesses they often bring but also because they demand constant movement, preventing soldiers from being adequately clothed or reinforced. Such campaigns also strain the transportation of ammunition and provisions. Even the best- trained army cannot sustain prolonged winter campaigns without severe consequences. For these reasons, winter campaigns should generally be avoided, as they are among the most punishing and challenging forms of warfare. Yet, circumstances may arise where a general has no choice but to undertake them.

Reflecting on my own experience, I believe I have undertaken more winter campaigns than any general of this era, and it may be useful to outline the motivations behind these decisions. In 1740, following the death of Emperor Charles VI, Silesia held only two Austrian regiments. Determined to assert my family's rightful claims over this duchy, I launched a winter campaign, aiming to capitalize on the advantageous conditions and quickly advance toward the Neiss. Had I waited until spring, the war front would likely have settled between Crossen and Glogau, necessitating three or four grueling campaigns to accomplish what we achieved with a single, well-timed march.

Another example is my winter campaign of 1742, when I attempted to protect the region from the Elector of Bavaria. That endeavor fell short, but not due to the season itself; rather, it failed because the French acted foolishly, and the Saxons proved untrustworthy. My third winter campaign, in the winter of 1741-42, became necessary when the Austrians invaded Silesia, forcing me to drive them back during a time of year when most would avoid warfare. In the winter of 1745-46, both the Austrians and the Saxons aimed to invade my hereditary lands, intending to wreak havoc. As was my custom, I decided to act preemptively and initiated a winter campaign within the heart of their territory, seizing the advantage by taking the war directly to them.

If I were to face similar conditions again, I would not hesitate to repeat such actions, and I would commend any of my generals who chose to follow this example. However, I must caution that without compelling reasons like these, a winter campaign should never be undertaken lightly.

For the logistics of winter campaigns, certain precautions are essential. Troops must be stationed as closely as possible in their cantonments, concentrating their strength in larger villages or towns whenever feasible. Ideally, two or three regiments of cavalry, mixed with infantry, should be housed together if the village is large enough to accommodate them. On some occasions, as when the Prince of Anhalt quartered his forces at Torgau, Eilenbourg, Meissen, and several other small Saxon towns, all infantry regiments may be gathered within a single town to maintain a more cohesive force, with the general remaining nearby in an encampment.

When we approach enemy territory, a rendezvous point should be established for all troops, who will then proceed in multiple columns. At the moment of any critical movement, whether preparing to storm enemy quarters or advancing to confront the enemy directly, the troops should arrange themselves in battle formation. In such circumstances, they may remain in open fields overnight, each company lighting large fires to endure the cold. Yet, these maneuvers demand great endurance, and their duration must be minimized. Swift, decisive action is key in winter warfare. Hesitation is a luxury we cannot afford; plans must be formed with boldness and executed with unwavering resolve.

If possible, winter campaigns should be avoided in regions dotted with fortified towns, as the season's constraints prevent a prolonged siege. Attempting to take well defended positions by surprise is often doomed to fail, as the logistical challenges of winter make it nearly impossible to sustain such efforts.

In the ideal scenario, troops should be allowed to rest as much as possible during the winter months. This time can be used to strengthen the army and make any necessary preparations so that when spring arrives, our forces can move out with a renewed advantage over the enemy.

These principles outline the key aspects of large-scale maneuvers in winter warfare, as comprehensively as I am able to explain. I have endeavored to make these guidelines as clear as possible. If any part seems ambiguous, I welcome you to communicate these concerns to me, so that I may either elaborate further or acknowledge if your insights exceed my own.

Through my experiences, limited as they may be, I have come to understand that war is a complex art, one that can never be fully mastered. It continually rewards those who study it with dedication, offering fresh insights to those who remain attentive. If this account encourages my officers to deepen their understanding of military science, I shall consider my time well spent. Such knowledge opens the surest path to glory, allowing men to lift their names from obscurity, achieving renown, and securing a legacy of immortal fame through bold and distinguished deeds.

Thank You for Reading

You've Just Read a Piece of the Greatest Library Ever Rebuilt

Thank you for reading.

This book is one of thousands we're restoring, reimagining, and translating as part of the **Modern Library of Alexandria** — a global movement to preserve and share humanity's most important ideas.

What was once lost to fire and time is now rising again — not just as memory, but as living, breathing knowledge, freely accessible to all.

What You Can Do Next:

- **Keep Reading** - Explore more legendary works in print, audiobook, or digital at LibraryofAlexandria.com.

- **Build Your Own Library** - Every title is available at true printing cost — paperback, hardcover, or collector's boxset.

- **Spread the Light** - Share this book. Support the mission to translate every timeless work into every language.

By finishing this book, you've already taken part in something extraordinary.

Join us at LibraryofAlexandria.com

Together, we're rebuilding the greatest library the world has ever known.

With gratitude,

The Modern Library of Alexandria Team

Visit:

www.libraryofalexandria.com

Or scan the code below:

www.ingramcontent.com/pod-product-compliance
Lightning Source LLC
Chambersburg PA
CBHW051838020726
47502CB00005B/1850